THE MAN WHO LIVED BY NIGHT

The Man Who Lived by Night

A Stewart Hoag Mystery

David Handler

This is a work of fiction. Names, characters, places, events, and incidents either are the product of the author's imagination or are used fictitiously. Any resemblance to actual persons, living or dead, businesses, companies, events, or locales is entirely coincidental.

ISBN: 979-8-3372-0543-4

This edition published in 2025 by MysteriousPress.com/Open Road Integrated Media, Inc.
180 Maiden Lane
New York, NY 10038
www.openroadmedia.com

For Helen Tucker Handler—
Miss New Jersey, 1919, or thereabouts

THE MAN WHO LIVED BY NIGHT

I'm the shadow man
A stranger in my own strange land
I'm the shadow man. Here I am.
The sun here, it never shines
There are no directions upon the signs
Always on the outside
Always looking in
I'm the shadow man.

—from the song by Tristam Scarr

"I am whoever they want me to be. If they want me to be a shit-kicking rock 'n' roll rebel, I am one. If they want me to be a drugged-out, decadent bleedin' millionaire, or a war protester, or a stud, or a poet, or a god, I am one. I am whoever they want. I am no one."

—from an interview with Tristam Scarr in *Playboy* magazine, May, 1973

CHAPTER ONE

Tris Scarr lied to me from the beginning. He promised me his limousine would meet my plane at Heathrow to drive me out to Gadpole, his place in Surrey. There was no limo. There was no message for me. There was no phone listing in Surrey for a Scarr, T. I was on my own. And I was not surprised. That was Tris Scarr for you. It wasn't for no reason that an entire generation of rock 'n' roll fans, myself included, knew the lead singer of Us simply as T. S.

I phoned Blakes to see if they had a room, and they did. A taxi took me there. It was the evening rush hour, and raining hard. That didn't stop Lulu, my basset hound, from insisting on a whiff. I rolled down my window. She planted her back paws firmly in my groin, stuck her large black nose out into the wet, fumy air, and snuffled happily. This was her first trip to London. She'd been looking forward to it.

Blakes is a small, quiet hotel on a small, quiet street in South Kensington. I've always liked the place, even though it has gotten chic lately. Merilee and I spent our honeymoon there. I liked it even more when I found out Mr. Tristam Scarr had an account there. I got a cozy room on the top floor in the back. There was a terrace. After I hung up my trench coat and Borsalino, I ordered smoked salmon sandwiches and a pot of tea from room service. Then I phoned the barman. I was working my way through the single malts that year. We decided he'd send up an aged Glenmorangie.

Next I phoned Jay Weintraub, T. S.'s lawyer in New York, and told him we had a problem.

"So he forgot to send a car," Jay soothed. "Not such a big—"

"If it was a priority he would have remembered."

"It is. Look, Hoagy, this is T. S. He's a unique, complex individual. He's been about the most famous rock personality in the world for over twenty years. You got to make allowances for people like that."

"You know what you get when you make allowances for people like that, Jay?"

"What?"

"A book that no one can be proud of."

"I don't see that happening with a writer of your caliber involved."

I let him have that one.

"Give him a chance, Hoagy. Be patient. T. S. has a hard time trusting people, with everything he's been through. They told me, I mean, you got a rep for being able to handle the tough ones."

"If they're genuinely serious about going through with it."

"He is. I know he is. He's ready to take the step. Bombshells he's got. Between you and me, I think he misses the limelight. And the money doesn't hurt."

The publisher was putting up $1.95 million for Tris Scarr's life story. I was getting a sliver of the pie, plus expenses, to help him tell it.

"I'll call Gadpole," offered Jay. "See if I can straighten this out. He'll get in touch with you. Hang out. It . . . it may not be *right* away."

"When, Jay?"

"Soon."

"When, Jay?"

"I don't know, okay? Just chill out. Please?"

I split the salmon sandwiches with Lulu. She had water with hers. I washed down mine with the tea and a short glass of Glenmorangie. It wasn't the worst scotch I'd ever tasted. Possibly, it was even better than the Glenlivet.

I drew myself a bubble bath. Next to clotted cream, baths are the best part of being in England. The tubs are actually long enough to lie down in. I've never understood the point of short American tubs, other than to drown small, loud children in. I poured myself another Glenmorangie, climbed in, and oozed down, down, down into it.

I didn't mind hanging out. Merilee, my ex-wife, happened to be arriving in a couple of days to play Tracy Lord in a revival of *The Philadelphia Story* at the Haymarket. Anthony Andrews of *Brideshead Revisited* was starring opposite her as C. K. Dexter Haven. There had been a rumor in Liz Smith's column before I left that Merilee and her new husband, that fabulously hot young playwright Zack something, weren't getting along. He was not making the trip with her.

I lay there in the tub, sipping my single malt and wondering. Wondering if she'd be happy to see me. Wondering what, if anything, would happen between us now that I sort of had my juices back. *Merilee.* We had fallen for each other in that fine, first flush of our own successes. She was Merilee Nash, Joe Papp's newest, loveliest darling. I was Stewart Hoag, that tall, dashing author of that fabulously successful first novel, *Our Family Enterprise*—the man who the *New York Times* had called "the first major new literary voice of the eighties." God, we were cute. And she stayed cute. Won a Tony for the Mamet play. An Oscar for the Woody Allen movie. Time put her on its cover. Me, I dried up. No juices—of any kind. No second novel. No marriage. I crashed. But that was behind me now. These days I was as happy as a man whose best days are behind him can be. I was even, at long last, working on a second novel. But it was coming in drips, not waves. Possibly, I'd have to finish living it before I could finish writing it. Possibly, I'd even have to grow up a little. In the meantime, I got by as a ghost. I'm ideally suited to my second, somewhat less dignified career as a ghostwriter—partly because celebrity memoirs are more fiction than anything else, partly because as a former luminary I have something in common with my subjects that the lunch-pail ghosts don't. What was it Norma said in *Sunset Boulevard*? "Great stars have great pride." Yeah. That pretty much covers it.

Of course, I have encountered one small occupational hazard. A ghost is a seeker of celebrity secrets, past and present. As it happens, there's often someone around who doesn't want those secrets dug up. I carry a pen, not a gun. Trouble is not my business. But my business can be trouble.

I ate dinner in the hotel, just in case T. S. called. I wore my navy blue Ferre suit with a starched white shirt, silver cuff links, maroon-and-white polka-dot bow tie and calf-leather braces. I looked like a million bucks. The hush when Lulu and I descended into the plush basement dining room was perceptible.

Chris Reeve was dining there with a stunning blonde. In town to make *Superman Eleven*, no doubt. He and Merilee did a play in Williamstown one summer, and I had learned that his only off-camera superpower was dullness. I ducked into the tiny bar only to be cornered by a Pittsburgh steel heir who assured me we'd chucked spears against each other on an Ivy League playing field a couple of decades before. I didn't remember him, but these days I find I don't remember much. The novel came up. He'd loved it. I bought him a drink. Or, T. S. did.

I got a corner table, where I tucked away duck liver pâté, lamb chops and a bottle of Côtes du Rhône. Lulu had a little grilled red snapper. I finished off with a pear tart, coffee and Calvados. Lulu had a little more snapper. No call came from T. S. We took a turn through the tidy, orderly streets of South Ken. The rain had let up. It was misty and gloomy out now. I like gloomy. Gloomy is deep. Gloomy is profound. Clear skies are for other people. Clear skies are for volleyball players and arbitrageurs and screenwriters. Lulu was getting into London. She sniffed gleefully at every bush and tree and lamppost, and got muddy paws and ears for her trouble. We went to bed late. Still no call.

The next morning I headed for Jermyn Street. At Floris I bought my cologne and talc. At Turnbull and Asser I bought a new shawl-collared target-dot silk robe. Merilee had stolen my old one. I always did have trouble holding onto my clothes, since she looked so much better in them than I did. The young, rakish T & A clerk, whose name was Nigel, also sold me some white shirts, after he gave up trying to sell me those gaudy striped ones. From there I strolled over to Savile Row. At Strickland's, Mr. Tricker fitted me for a sixteen-ounce gray cheviot wool suit, once he got done sniffing at my Ferre. While I was there I ordered a new pair of cordovan brogans from Maxwell's. There was still no call when I got back to the hotel. I spent the afternoon out on my terrace in the fog with Lulu, a blanket, a pot of tea, the Glenmorangie and *Six Decades*, a collection of Irwin Shaw short stories which I reread every couple of years to remind myself what good writing is. No call. I went to see the new Ayckbourn play. Still no call.

It woke me in the middle of the night.

"It seems there was a mix-up." The voice was soft and well educated. There was no trace of the famous Liverpudlian accent. Jay had warned me T. S. didn't actually talk the way people thought. That was put on. "I thought you were arriving next week, you see."

I said absolutely nothing. Just listened to him breathe. It sounded like the receiver was stuck halfway down his throat.

"A mix-up, you see," he repeated, a bit uneasily now.

I still said nothing.

Neither did he. Until, after a very long silence, he finally said, "I'm sorry."

"I'll be on the morning train to Guildford. Have someone meet me there."

"Yes. Right. Of course."

"Isn't there something else you wanted to say?"

"Such as?"

"Such as that there was no mix-up. That you purposely forgot so you could test my boiling point, and that you won't do it again."

He chuckled. It was the mad, malevolent chuckle of the Jolly Buganeer from *Skullduggery*, the Us pirate-theme album that sold eight or nine million copies in the early seventies, and was made into that vomitous Ken Russell movie.

"It wouldn't do to push me, mate," he snarled. Now he sounded like the tough teddy who punched his way out of Liverpool-total transformation. "I push back, and bloody hard."

"Fine. Push someone else back. I quit."

I hung up on him. Then I waited for him to call back. Stars always do when I hang up on them. They aren't used to being treated that way. It challenges them. They like it.

I let it ring three times before I answered it. I listened to more heavy breathing. And then, finally:

"I won't do it again."

"Thank you. Good night, Tristam."

"Good night, Hogarth."

I turned over and went back to sleep. Our collaboration had begun.

A claret-colored Rolls-Royce Silver Cloud met me at the Guildford train station. The uniformed chauffeur was in his forties, beefy, red-faced and moustached. I helped him load my bags in the trunk, then Lulu and I sank into the back seat. There was a bar back there. Also a television, a refrigerator, a lot of dark wood and dove gray leather, and a glass divider, which was shut. The ride wasn't bad, if you're into total comfort.

The outskirts of Guildford were dotted with ugly new housing and shopping developments. That's one thing the British do even worse than we do. But soon there was little more than beech-woods and heathland and crumbling stone fences. And peaceful storybook villages. Shere. Gomshall. Wotton. The ramparts of a ruined Norman castle stood guard at the top of a hill outside of Dorking. At Bletchingley, we turned into a narrow, hedge-lined road, and the chauffeur opened the divider.

"That'll be Place Farm on your right, sir," he intoned, as we cruised past a stone castle so colossal even Donald Trump would be content to retire there. "Anne of Cleves lived here. Henry the Eighth gave it to her when they divorced in the year 1540."

"Just think what she'd have gotten if Marvin Mitchelson had been around then."

"Sir?"

"Nothing."

In another mile or so the hedged road ended at a wrought-iron gate. Here, two guards in business suits were on duty. One of them opened the trunk of the Rolls and began to paw through my bags. The other asked me to please get out of the car.

"We walking the rest of the way?" I asked.

"Routine security, sir," he replied. "Nothing personal."

The accent was American. So was the suit. Sears—the Arnie Palmer collection. He patted me down for hidden weapons, then said I could get back in. The other guard slammed the trunk shut. The gates swung slowly open. And into the realm—the secure realm—of Tristam Scarr we drove.

The road was crushed gravel and lined with beeches. It took us past meadows, past woods, past terraced gardens, past a lake. Then it cut through a clustering of little stone buildings—houses for staff and security people, stables, garages, a chapel. Almost a village unto itself. It was hard to imagine driving for so long without ever leaving your own property. Hard to imagine, but nice. A covered bridge took us over a stream and then there was Gadpole. It was an eighteenth-century brick manor house, three stories high with a glassed dome at its center. I doubt there were more than sixty rooms.

"Rock pays," I said.

"It does indeed, sir," agreed the chauffeur. "Handsomely."

Two more guards were on the front door. There were fourteen of them altogether, I was to learn. All of them retired FBI agents.

The housekeeper wore a sweater and pleated skirt of matching bottle green cashmere and knobby brown oxfords. She was in her sixties, plump, pink-cheeked and silver-haired. She smiled and fluttered a hand at me as I got out.

"Yes, yes, Mister Hoag," she called out cheerily. "Please do come in. He'll not be awake for hours, but he's asked me to make you comfortable. I am Pamela."

"It's Hoagy," I said as we went inside. "And this is Lulu."

"Why hello, Miss Lulu."

Lulu promptly rolled over on the polished marble floor of

the entrance hall, four paws up, to be petted. She has a knack for buttering up anyone who might be in a position to slip her tasty morsels.

Delighted, Pamela knelt with a refined grunt and patted Lulu's belly. To Lulu she said, "What a sweet little thing you are." To me she said, "My, her breath is rather . . ."

"She has funny eating habits," I informed her. "As I'm sure you'll find out."

Gadpole wasn't an understated house. The entrance hall was two stories high and encrusted with ornate molding. A curving marble staircase wide enough to accommodate a Range Rover led up to the second floor. A tall doorway framed by columns and an angular pediment opened into the immense living room, where there was plenty more wedding-cake plasterwork, and a ceiling painted with nymphs and swans. The furniture was lacquered Louis XV. The tables were gilded with leaf patterns, the chairs intricately carved and upholstered in red silk. It was all exceedingly rococo and, seemingly, genuine. On the walls were a lot of formal portraits of a lot of dead English people. On the floor were richly colored Persian rugs. It wasn't at all the sort of place I'd expected from a man who once dropped his black leather pants in front of eighteen thousand screaming fans at Madison Square Garden and dared the police to arrest him. (They did.) It was more the kind of place I imagined Truman Capote would have lived in if he'd been born a peer. And who's to say he wasn't.

Lulu sneezed. She was shivering. So was her master.

The house was as warm and snug as a meat locker.

"I've had the west wing guest suite made up per your instructions," said Pamela. "I do hope you'll be comfortable."

"If there's heat there we'll be fine."

She chuckled. "You American visitors are always cold."

"And Mr. Scarr?"

She frowned, bit her lower lip fretfully. "I'm afraid Mr. Scarr feels very little."

The west wing guest suite was on the second floor, and so far down the long, carpeted hallway that it was in a different century. This one. The sitting room was masculine and clubby, right down to the hunting scene prints on the walls and the nicely worn leather sofa and armchairs grouped around the fireplace, which was, mercifully, lit. The typewriter I'd asked for was set up on a massive walnut desk in front of the tall windows that overlooked Gadpole's maze. Clearly, whoever had positioned it there had never tried to write a second novel. Pamela opened a wardrobe cupboard to reveal a television, videocassette recorder, stereo system and small refrigerator. There were bookcases full of interesting-looking books and a sideboard full of interesting-looking bottles.

In the bedroom there was a huge four-poster bed and another wardrobe, this one for clothes. Someone had already brought up my bags.

"I'll be in the kitchen if you want breakfast," said Pamela.

"Thank you. Lulu will lead me to it."

Actually, Lulu had claimed the leather chair closest to the fire and showed no signs of ever wanting to move. Possibly she preferred this to our dingy little fifth-floor walk-up on West Ninety-Third Street. Possibly she wasn't the only one.

"Your rooms will be made up daily," Pamela went on gaily. "Anything you need cleaned or laundered please leave by the door, and I'll have it taken care of. I do hope you'll be happy here, Hoagy."

"I think I can manage for the next twenty or thirty years."

There was a Macallan single malt on the sideboard that was almost as old as I am. It was certainly a lot smoother. As I sampled it I unpacked the Fair Isle sweater vest I'd had knitted for Lulu when she had bronchitis one winter. I didn't want her developing breathing problems again. She snores when she has them. I know this because she likes to sleep on my head. She wriggled gratefully into it. I put her bowls down in the bathroom. Also the cases of the only canned food she'll eat—Nine Lives mackerel for cats and very strange dogs. Then I hung up my clothes and decided to explore.

There wasn't much else in the west wing besides closed doors. The east wing was closed off entirely. The stairs up to the third floor and the dome terminated at a small landing, where there was a set of heavy double doors. Closed. Here sat another guard, reading a copy of *USA Today*. He looked up at me. He didn't smile.

"Mr. Scarr's room?" I asked, glancing at the doors.

"And recording studio. And kitchen. The works. He's got it all over Hef. You'll be Hoag."

I nodded.

"He's asleep now. Or doesn't want to be bothered. Later."

Downstairs I found a library, a formal dining room, a paneled billiards room and a grand ballroom that dwarfed the living room. A Knicks game could go unnoticed in there. Lulu was the one who found the kitchen, where Pamela was rinsing berries in the sink and humming. It was a modern kitchen, and not small. There were three refrigerators and a commercial-size hooded range.

"Have you eaten?"

"No, ma'am."

"Then pour yourself some coffee and sit," she commanded, indicating a cluttered country pine table. "He'll not be stirring for hours and hours. He only lives by night, you see."

"Like Count Dracula?"

"You've seen him then?"

"We've never met."

But I knew him. Just about everyone in America had since 1964, when he first appeared on *The Ed Sullivan Show*, his scowling, pockmarked face thrust brazenly forward at the camera, nostrils flared with impudence, voice a raspy primal scream. That night he sang Us's hit version of the Little Richard song, "Great Gosh Almighty." There would be so many more hits through the years—"Come On Over, Baby," "More for Me," "This Must Be Love," "New Age," "Miss Eloise," "We're Double Trouble," "For Johnny Baughan." Sure I knew him. He was T. S., full of talent and anger and himself. Strutting. Preening. Pointing at the audience. Condemning it. Alongside him there on the Sullivan stage stood Rory Law, his blond hair an uncombed mop, his snaggled teeth working on his lower lip as he fired off the brutal guitar chops that gave Us its distinctive sound. T. S. and Rory. Boyhood friends. Co-founders of Us. Popularly known as Double Trouble. Behind them, Puppy Johnson attacked the drums, sweating, grinning. Puppy Johnson, the man who, by way of Monroe, Louisiana, became Britain's first black rock star. The man who the British press labeled "the wild man of Borneo" for his drumming style and his lifestyle. Thumping away next to him on bass was Derek Gregg, the tall handsome one with the choirboy face and the angelic voice.

They were nasty and rude. They were rebels. Together, the four of them rode the second wave that washed ashore in America after the Beatles hit. That was the one that brought the Rolling Stones, the Who, the Animals. Us would last as long as anyone. They would outlast rhythm and blues, rockabilly, acid rock, reggae, heavy metal and disco. Their sound was their own, and no one did anything better. But that wasn't the only reason they got as much attention as they did. They were the bad boys. They took too many drugs, threw too many punches, used up too many women. They fought with the world and with each other. Always, it seemed, there was feuding and controversy. Violence. Scandal. Death. Only a year after that first Sullivan appearance Puppy Johnson was jailed in Little Rock, Arkansas for the statutory rape of a fifteen-year-old white girl. The group was banished from America. Two years later Puppy was dead from a drug overdose. The band went on. Triumphed. Broke up. Reformed. Triumphed again until that ghastly night in Atlanta's Omni auditorium, summer of '76, when Rory Law was gunned down on stage by a former disciple of Charles Manson. T. S. went on alone from there. Tried performing solo after the release of his album *Shadow Man.* But when someone threw a lit firecracker up on stage one night, and it exploded next to him, he walked off and never came back. He bought Gadpole and went into seclusion. After John Lennon's assassination he hired a full-time force of security guards to protect him. He seldom came out now. In fact, he had not been seen in public in over ten years.

Sure I knew him. Long ago, Tris Scarr had been my idol—the one after Mantle and before Mailer. Tris Scarr had provided the soundtrack for my coming of age.

Only, I didn't know him. No one did. He was, as Jay Weintraub had said, a complex man, a man of different faces, of contradictions, of anger. A man whose personal turmoil *was* rock 'n' roll. He had gleefully cultivated high-class friends and sophisticated tastes, yet at the same time blasted those who had money and privilege. He had partied and drugged and wrecked hotel rooms, yet was considered a sensitive poet and a serious intellectual. His stormy love life had consumed some of the most famous beauties of the past three decades, most notably Tulip, the London supermodel—The Mod Bod—whom he eventually married. He was T. S. He had seen it all and done it all—to himself and to others. He was a man who had stories to tell, and he'd agreed to tell them. The feuds. The women. The drugs. It all.

"Bacon and eggs do, Mr. Hoag?" asked Pamela.

"Always have. And it's Hoagy. Please."

"As in Carmichael?"

"As in the cheese steak."

She frowned. "I see." She went into the pantry and returned with eggs and a slab of bacon. "How do you like your eggs, Hoagy?"

"The same way I like everything else," I replied, stirring my coffee. "Soft-boiled."

CHAPTER TWO

It was my fault we got lost in the maze.

Lulu hadn't wanted to go in there. She was having too much fun barking at the herd of deer nibbling on the grass at the edge of the woods. She even made a few of them bound off in terror. It was the happiest I'd seen her since she treed a baby squirrel in Riverside Park. But I insisted, and I'm bigger. Grudgingly, she waddled along next to me through the carefully pruned geometric corridors of ten-foot-high box hedges. First right, then left. Then left, then right. I had never been in a maze before. I liked it in there, and the notion we wouldn't be able to find our way out never occurred to me—I assumed Lulu would know how to, being a dog. I assumed wrong. To give her credit, she tried. But all she found was one dead end after another. Ultimately, all paths led to the gazebo in the maze's center, where there was a cast iron table and chairs and a metal strongbox. On the box was printed the words OPEN ME. I did. Inside it was a flare gun and a note: FIRE ME. Twenty minutes later the chauffeur arrived.

"I'm quite embarrassed," I said, apologetically.

"Don't be, sir. Happens to all of our guests."

"Even when they have a dog with them?"

"That is a new one, actually"

The chauffeur cheated. He had a map. We came out on the other side, where T. S.'s car collection was stored in converted stables. He liked Alfas. He owned two—a '31 1750 Zagato Grand Sport and a '59 Giulietta Sprint Coupe Racer. He liked Ferraris. He had a mouthwatering red '59 Pininfarina and a '67 275 GTB four-cam. He liked nice cars, period. There was a '52 Aston Martin Lagonda cabriolet, a '55 Mercedes 300SL gull-wing, a '39 Packard Dutch Darrin convertible, a '64 Studebaker Gran Turismo Hawk, a '72 Maserati Ghibli spyder, a '52 Bentley R-Type Continental, a '56 T-Bird, a '57 Corvette. There were others. He even had a Delorean.

"Nice collection," I observed to the chauffeur, who had gone back to rubbing the Silver Cloud with a chamois. "If you like this sort of thing."

"Mr. Scarr does, sir," he replied pleasantly. "He does indeed."

I stuck out my hand. "It's Hoagy.

His hand was meaty and strong. "Jack, sir. Pleased to meet you."

"Been with him long?"

"A number of years. Yessir. Relatively quiet, this. Not like before. The girls used to paint lipstick kisses all over his car. Throw themselves in its path in the hope of meeting him. Plenty of goings on."

"You must have quite a few stories. I'd like to hear them sometime for his book."

"I'm only a chauffeur, sir. You flatter me."

"It won't hurt a bit—scout's honor."

He shrugged his heavy shoulders noncommittally. And said, "May I be so bold as to offer you a suggestion, sir?"

"Fire away."

He stepped toward me until his face was very close to mine.

His breath smelled of beer and pickled onions and either very strong cheese or very old socks. "Don't look into the past."

"That's my job—looking into the past."

"Then I wouldn't look too closely."

There was a hint of menace in his voice now. At my heels, Lulu growled softly.

"Any particular reason?" I asked.

"I'll put it this way. You look like a bright young gent . . ."

"Not so young."

"It wouldn't be bright."

A threat, no question.

I nodded. "Duly noted. Up this road get me back?"

"Yessir."

"By the way—how does the Delorean run?"

"It doesn't."

It was dusk by the time we reached the house. After I fed Lulu I phoned the Haymarket. Merilee had arrived, but was presently in rehearsal. I left word where she could reach me. Then I popped open a bottle of lager and watched part eight of a sixteen-part series on BBC 1 called *Giant Worms of the Sea*. Whoever thinks British television has it all over American TV has never actually watched any. Then Pamela phoned to say dinner would be served in fifteen minutes. I asked if we were dressing. We were not.

The only light in the dining room came from the silver candelabra at the center of the huge dining table. Only one place was set. Mine. There was grilled rabbit and silver serving dishes of fried potatoes and buttered brussels sprouts waiting for me. A bucket held a chilled Sancerre. I dived in. It was delicious. It was also a tiny bit creepy eating there alone in the cold, dark dining hall, surrounded by more portraits of more dead English people, the only sound that of my teeth tearing into the bunny wabbit. I knew there had to be cooks and maids around, but Pamela administered them so discreetly they were never in evidence. I was grateful when she finally came in to ask if everything was all right.

"Excellent," I assured her. "Most flavorful rabbit I've ever tasted."

"You've Jack to thank for its freshness. He's our gamekeeper. It's his hobby—pheasant, quail, hare. A fine shot, he is. Care for dessert?"

"No, thanks."

"Coffee then?"

"If it's no bother," I said. "Wouldn't it be easier if I ate in the kitchen?"

That tickled her. She laughed. "Formality makes you Americans so uncomfortable. Yes, yes, of course. You may eat where you wish. Was the time all right?"

"When do *you* eat?"

She reddened slightly in the flickering candlelight, heightening her lovely complexion. "Seven."

"Seven it is then."

She started back to the kitchen for my coffee, stopped. "I intended to ask you—have you a favorite food?"

"Only licorice ice cream."

"I'm so sorry."

"Not as sorry as I am."

The guard at the royal bedchamber door was a different one, but he didn't smile at me either. Just nodded and knocked. A voice answered from inside. I went in.

"Hiya, Hogarth," Tris Scarr said dully, as he shuffled slowly toward me in backless slippers, his posture stooped. "Come in. I was just eating m'breakfast."

Someone once described Tris Scarr as the only man alive who

could look angry by the mere physical act of breathing. It was his nostrils—the way they flared. But he didn't look angry now. He looked weary and weak and sallow. His eyes were heavy-lidded and pouched, his pitted, unshaven face gaunt. He wore a loosely belted green paisley dressing gown. Below it, his bare legs were skinny and pale. Blue veins protruded from the tops of his feet above his slippers. He was smaller than I expected he'd be—five feet eight tops, and he couldn't have weighed more than 130. His hairless chest was positively concave. He still wore his black hair long and scraggly, only now it was streaked with gray. I hadn't, I realized, seen a photograph of him in several years—there hadn't been any photographs since he'd moved to Gadpole. In some ways, he still looked like that same rude, naughty boy of the swingin' sixties. In other ways he looked much older than forty-five. It was as if his body was in the process of skipping middle age entirely.

He stuck out his hand. It was delicate and unsteady, the fingers yellowed from chain-smoking unfiltered Gauloises. I shook it. He had less grip than my grandmother, who is 90.

The room was immense and round and several stories high, what with the glass dome over it. In the middle was a sunken island of low sofas arranged around a big square coffee table crowded with sketch pads, note pads, books, packages of Gauloises, ashtrays, bottles of pills, more bottles of pills, a wine bucket with a half-empty bottle of sauterne in it, and a half-eaten jar of baby food that had a spoon stuck in it. Strained liver. Goes great with sauterne. Especially for breakfast. There was a bedroom through a half-open door, and a small, modern kitchen. His soundproofed recording studio was on the other side of a glass partition. In there was an old upright piano, an organ, guitars, and a full drum kit. Beyond it was a booth with tape machines in it.

There were lamps, and they were on, but silk scarves were draped over the shades. No music was playing. T. S. never listened to music at any time during our collaboration. The only sound came from the grandfather clock next to the door.

I sat down in one of the sofas. He coughed—a phlegmy cough—lit a cigarette with a disposable lighter, poured himself some sauterne and didn't offer me any. Then he sat down across the table from me and stared at me. And kept staring at me. He wasn't what you'd call warm. He wasn't what you'd call *there.*

Finally, he cleared his throat and said, "You don't use a tape recorder."

"I will. I thought we'd want to get acquainted first."

He absently flicked the ash from his cigarette. It landed next to him on the sofa. There were, I noticed, dozens of burn marks there in the upholstery. "Acquainted?"

"Acquainted."

"If you wish." He yawned and sipped his wine. "Have you questions then?"

I glanced over at his studio. "I didn't know you were still recording."

He shrugged. "Personal things. Different things."

"Will you be releasing any of it?"

"Through with all of that. Don't care if people hear it."

"You sound like J. D. Salinger."

He brightened, though not a lot. "The American writer. Yes. I've read he's written dozens of books but he won't let anyone read them until he dies. I admire that."

"Why?"

"Because people are bloody fools."

I didn't fight him on that one. "You're through performing, too?"

Another cigarette ash landed on the sofa. This one began to

smolder. "Rockers don't grow up. We just grow old, y'know? I've had it with that. No more pretending I'm still T. S. I want to write, paint, be m'self. Rock 'n' roll music comes from being young, from being angry." He looked around at his dome. "Not from this."

"What do you want from this book? Understanding? Appreciation? Respect?"

"Bugger that. I don't care what anyone thinks of me anymore. I'm looking to close the door and be done with it. Walk off into the sunset like John Fucking Wayne."

"He once called you a sick limey fairy."

"Then I must have been doing something right, wasn't I? I wasn't there to give 'em a cup of tea and tuck 'em into bed, mate. I was there to shake 'em up. Turn up the heat. Rock 'n' roll, it's their last chance, isn't it?"

"Whose?"

"The teenies, before they go off to be everything they don't want to be. Just like their mums and dads before 'em."

"Is that your philosophy of rock music?"

"There is no philosophy. Just the music. That's all there is. See, I . . ." He trailed off.

"Go on," I urged him. "Please."

"I didn't want . . . I *don't* want to end up like Elvis."

"Fat and dead?"

"Before that."

"Fat and semi-alive?"

"I met him once. When we played at Las Vegas in . . . perhaps it was the '69 tour. Or was it '71? Can't remember. A blur, it is. We went to see his midnight show at one of those hotel-casinos. It was . . ." He shuddered, horrified by the memory. "Pathetic. There he was with his fat face, bursting out of his white sequined trousers. Couldn't sing for shit. But his fans, they were screaming for him like he was still the king and they were still hot and nasty little teenies. They weren't, you see. They were old and fat themselves. Housewives. Lorry drivers in green leisure suits." He shuddered again. "Afterward, we met him in his suite."

"How was he?"

"Zonked. Totally zonked. Didn't know who we were. Didn't know who he was. It shook me. I went back to my room and wrote a song about it."

"*Shoot the Old Hound Dog.* I remember it."

"Elvis, he was *my* idol."

The cigarette ash continued to smolder on the sofa next to him.

"How do you see yourself now?"

"See myself?"

"Are you a hero? A victim? A survivor?"

He shrugged. "I'm T. S. I'm here. This is now. Tomorrow . . ."

"Tomorrow?"

"Tomorrow there'll be another now." He cocked his head and cupped an ear with one hand, as if he'd heard the sound of distant drumbeats. I'd heard nothing. "That's lovely, isn't it? 'Another now.'" Pleased, he reached for a pen and scribbled it down on a pad. Then he tossed the pad back on the table. "Sorry. If I don't get them on paper these days, I forget them."

"You aren't alone," I assured him. "Any regrets?"

"Only that I'm not nineteen."

"Why nineteen?"

"It was good then. It was the best. Oscar Wilde, he once said that living well is the best revenge. Well, Oscar Wilde never got up on a stage and played rock 'n' roll music. It was good then. All of it. Me, Rory, the mates, the music. I . . . m'body is failing me now, Hogarth. Plumbing's ruined all the way down the line. Can't eat. Can't shit. Can't even take a bleedin' piss. Have to sit in a bleedin' diaper half the time. Take stomach pills, heart pills. I'm *old*, mate. Old before m'time. We all are—those of us who are left. A lot of the mates are already gone. Rory. Puppy Brian. Bonzo. Moon. Hendrix. I probably haven't much time left m'self . . . Nineteen. It was good then. Playin' all night for 'em in the little clubs. Playin' for the love of it. Pullin' chicks. Feelin' good. No hassles. No Lord Harry . . ." His features darkened.

"Lord Harry?"

"Smack. Heroin."

"It was rumored you were an addict. I never knew for sure."

"Two years of supercharged heaven, followed by the price. Still paying that. Anything hard would kill me now." He had a spoonful of the strained liver and shook his head. "It's all different now. Used to be you'd park your bum on a stool and they'd turn on the machine and you'd have a recording by morning. Now it takes months and months. Now it's Moogs and sixteen bleedin' channels. Sound paintings, they call 'em. It's not about *music.* And touring, Christ, it's not about music either. It's about laser light shows, and private jets and personal bleedin' masseuses, and videos on the MTV. Do you watch that MTV over there?"

"No, I have goldfish."

"Rock's big business now, mate. That's the total opposite of what it's supposed to be about."

"You helped make it that way."

"I know that. Sick about it, too."

"You could always give the money back," I suggested, grinning.

Briefly, his famous nostrils flared. Then he relaxed and let out a short, harsh laugh. "Not *that* sick."

"If you want to walk away then why don't you just do it? Why bother to write this book?"

He scratched at his stubbly chin, thought that over. "Because

I need to say some things before I go. Because I'm tired of Pete Townshend telling everyone he's so bloody deep. Because . . . because I want to show them, all of them, what's really inside Tristam Scarr."

"I thought you didn't care what people thought of you anymore."

"I don't. I care what *I* think, see?"

"Yes, I believe I do. But before we go any further I have to tell you that your couch is on fire."

Very slowly, he turned and looked at the cushion next to him, which was most definitely in flames. His expression, or rather lack of it, didn't change. He just kept looking at the flames, until he calmly reached over with his bare hand and patted them out, seemingly oblivious to whatever in the way of heat or pain this might involve. Then he turned and focused on me once again.

"I need a couple of assurances from you," I said.

He narrowed his eyes at me. "Assurances?"

"Working on a memoir, a good one, can be very demanding. Not to mention tortuous."

"I want a good one." He said this to me like he was a spoiled kid picking out a bicycle. "I want the best one."

"Fine. Then I'm going to push the hell out of you. That's my job. I'm asking you to have faith in me. If I'm not satisfied, I have a reason for it. I don't want image from you. I don't want *People* magazine. I want *you.* I want to know what you were feeling and dreaming. I want to know what color the wallpaper was. It's going to be hard and draining and time-consuming. I'm going to be a pain in the ass at times. Jay said you're committed to seeing this through. I want to hear that from you, because if there's the slightest chance you're going to get tired of this after a few days then I'd just as soon not get started at all."

He frowned, puzzled. "Jay?"

"Jay Weintraub."

"Ah, the lawyer. Yes. How do you know him?"

"He hired me."

"I see. Well . . . Yes, you have that assurance, Hogarth. I'm yours. I'm not going anywhere, except to hell."

"The other assurance I need is that you'll be totally honest with me. You have to tell me the truth."

"The *truth*." He turned the word over aloud several times, as if it were a strange, metaphysical concept. "That will be the interesting part. So much of it has been lies through the years. Hasn't been, strictly speaking, *real*, y'know?"

"No, not exactly, but I'm still on New York time—give me a while to catch up. What do you mean by 'real'?"

"Real as in Derek, the teeny dreamboat—"

"Your bass player."

"—used to bugger muscular boys."

"Oh?"

"Real as in who he actually wanted to turd-burgle was Rory."

"He did?"

"Only Rory was fucking m'Tulip."

"He was?"

"Who I was actually married to for two bleedin' years before anyone was allowed to know about it. The truth . . ." He shook his head. "The truth never entered into it at all. Christ, *Puppy* . . ." He trailed off, reached for a cigarette and lit it from the stub of the first.

Myself, I managed not to salivate on my trousers. Tris Scarr had just dished up enough dirt for three best sellers, and he wasn't even warm yet. I cleared my throat, and said "Puppy?"

"He was killed, mate."

"An accidental overdose. I remember."

"That was no accident. He was done in. Don't you see?"

"No, I'm afraid I don't."

"Done in," he repeated, emphatically.

"You're suggesting that someone *murdered* Puppy Johnson?"

"I'm not suggestin' it. I'm sayin' it."

"But who?"

"Never found out. Never will now." He took a sip of his wine and narrowed his eyes at me again. "Need any more assurances, Hogarth?"

I smiled. "We're going to do just fine, Tristam. In fact, we're going to write ourselves one helluva book."

"The best. I want the best."

"And you shall have it."

"I'm accustomed to working from midnight to dawn. Can't seem to change. You mind?"

"Not at all. I can type during the day. Take care of the other interviews."

He frowned, confused. "Other interviews? I thought this was *my* book."

"It is, but other sources will spark your remembrances. Also provide us with some objectivity. Don't worry—I'll sift everything through your voice."

He nodded. "I see."

"Who might be of help?"

He took a long time answering that one. "There's Derek . . ."

"What's he up to these days?"

"He's being a toff in Bedford Square with his guns."

"Guns?"

"Antiques. He collects them."

"How about Tulip?"

He didn't answer me.

"Or your ex-manager?"

"Marco's running a disco these days. Tulip . . . she's running around on ceilings. Bonkers, she is. Found the Lord. Pastries, as well." He swiped at his nose with the back of his hand. "There aren't a lot of good feelings, mate. I reckon some of that's my fault. What I mean is, they may not want to talk."

"Leave that part to me," I told him. "I'll need a car. Either you can loan me one or I'll rent one and send Jay the bill. Up to you."

"I'm to pay for it?"

"Part of the deal."

"I see. In the contract, is it?"

"I can go down and get my copy if you—"

"No, no. Not necessary, Hogarth. I believe you. Just didn't know, you see. Feel free to take any of the cars."

"Thank you."

"The utility cars, of course. Not the show cars. The show cars are mine. Jack will give you the keys. He's the—"

"Chauffeur. We've met."

"Capable bloke. Was our roadie for a time. Anything else?"

"I'd like to be able to listen to your old records. Didn't bring mine."

"All of them?"

"If you have them."

"Oh, I have 'em," he assured me, getting slowly to his feet. Our talk seemed to have drained him. He shuffled over to a wall of bookcases, came back with a boxed set of Us record albums called *Completely Us*. "Collector's item. All electronically reprocessed. Getting three hundred pounds for it."

"I'll take good care of it." I took it from him. Together, we started for the door. "You know, I saw you play Shea Stadium on your second American tour, in '65." I could still see him jumping around on the Shea stage that night. Now he was out of breath from crossing the room.

He grinned crookedly at me. "Yes, I thought you looked

familiar—you were the one in the front row wearing blue jeans, right?"

"I meant . . . I mean, you were great. You guys were a great band."

"We were the best, mate." His nostrils flared. "And Michael Jagger can kiss m'bloody arse."

"Tomorrow, I'll bring my tape recorder."

Lulu was asleep in her chair before the fire. The message I was hoping for was waiting there on my desk, courtesy of Pamela, who'd also turned down my bed. Possibly I would have to take her back to New York with me.

I sat at the desk and made notes of my initial conversation with Tris Scarr. He was reserved and elusive and in charge. Which approach should I take with him? Buddy? Bully? Shrink? Which would work on him? Which would bring him to life on the page? Too soon to tell.

After I'd put on my new silk dressing gown and poured myself a Macallan I pulled out the very first Us album, *Great Gosh Almighty—It's Us*! For the cover, the four of them had formed a human pyramid in Hyde Park, wearing matching gold blazers without lapels, skinny black neckties and goofy faces. They were just boys—gawky, pimply boys. On the back cover was that very same human pyramid shot from behind. Har har. And some copy: *"Their names are Tris, Rory, Derek and Albert (though his mates call him Puppy). All London is talking about these four swinging young lads from up Liverpool way who play to the Mersey beat but their own way. They're mod. They're now. They're gear. They're Us!"*

I put the album on the stereo, and listened to the title cut. I've finally reached a point where I can hear rock from my youth and not be preoccupied by its evocations of school dances on gymnasium floors and sweaty, unsure rumblings in overheated cars. It's just music now, and this was fresh, joyous music, bursting with energy and exuberance. Tris's voice was a ballsy wail, Rory's chords sharp and scorching. Derek's bass was tight and steady underneath, Puppy drove them, his drum shots crisp as breadsticks. They were pure and full of juice, their sound uncompromised by the drugs and the years. They were good. It had been good then, he'd said.

I poured myself another scotch and turned the music down. Then I stretched out on the bed and called her. My heart began to pound when she said hello. It always does.

"So how's Anthony Andrews?" I asked.

"Just a total dreamboat," she replied in that very proper, very dizzy teenage-girl's voice that is hers and hers alone. "Also desperately in love."

"With. . . ?"

"Anthony Andrews. Hoagy, darling?"

"Yes, Merilee?"

"Hello."

"Hello yourself."

Lulu heard her voice over the phone. She always can. Don't ask me how. She came charging in from the living room, considered her chances of making it up onto the big four-poster bed, ruled them out, and barked. She has a mighty big bark for someone with no legs. I shushed her and hoisted her up. She dug in next to me and gazed expectantly at the phone.

"Actually, it's going unbelievably well so far," Merilee said. "Which is just as well—we open next week You'll come, won't you? To the opening."

"Love to."

"Good. I'll make sure there's tickets for you two at the box office."

"I have to tell you that Lulu's not much of a Philip Barry fan—she thinks he's strictly yesterday."

"She feel that way about her mommy, too?"

"Hardly. She speaks of you often, and in glowing terms. I'll see if I can get the night off. We'll have supper afterward. Or is there a party?"

"For you, I'll skip it," she said. "Unless, of course, you want to go."

"Let's not," I suggested.

"Let's not," she agreed. "So how's T. S.?"

"Not all there. Actually, I've never met anyone before who so aptly fits the phrase 'shell of a human being.' With the possible exception of myself, of course."

I waited for her to contradict me. She didn't. "I used to have his picture on my wall when I was at Miss Porter's," she said. "His jeans were so tight you could see the outline of his dinkus."

"I always figured you were more of a Derek Gregg type."

"Never, darling. *Everybody* liked him."

"Especially the boys," I advised, confidentially.

She gasped. "No, really?!"

"From the horse's mouth."

"Ooh, tell me more."

"Remember when Puppy Johnson died?"

"OD'd on liquor and pills, didn't he?"

"T. S. says he was murdered."

"I don't know about that one, Hoagy," she said skeptically. "There's always weirdness attached to major rock deaths. Some people believe that Jim Morrison is still alive somewhere, and that Brian Jones was actually murdered by the CIA. When I was shooting that thing in Tennessee with Sissy we went to Graceland one weekend. Some of Elvis's fans there think he's off living in a parallel universe. It's all a lot of baked beans, isn't it?"

"Most likely. I've missed your quaint little expressions."

"Besides, it was over twenty years ago," she pointed out.

"That may be true, but his chauffeur did threaten me tonight."

"Hoagy, you're not getting into the middle of something ugly and scary again, are you?"

"I certainly hope not."

"I worry about you sometimes."

"You do?" I asked, pleased at this. "Why?"

"You don't know when it's time to walk away."

"I'll take that as a compliment,"

"I gave it as a constructive criticism."

"Oh."

She cleared her throat. "Is there a novel?"

"I think so. There's something."

"That's wonderful, darling! I'm so glad."

"You might not be so glad when you hear what it's about."

"Why, what's it . . . Oh no, you're not doing something tacky and Nora Ephronish are you?"

"That'll be for the *Times* to decide."

She sighed. "Kind of funny, the two of us being here at the same time, isn't it?"

"Yeah. Funny."

"I always think of London as our city."

"I stayed at Blakes."

"You romantic fool."

"You got that half right."

"Which half?"

"Where are you staying?"

"A darling little mews house on Cromwell Road. I'm subletting from a British actress who's doing a movie in New York." She sighed again. "I don't know what it is about this city. I mean, it's most definitely not romantic. It's damp and gray and it smells of exhaust fumes and simply awful cologne."

"Merilee?"

"Yes, darling?"

"How's Zack?"

She hesitated. "Zack's home having some problems. We have that to talk about, too."

We were silent a minute.

"Darling?" This she said softly.

"Yes, Merilee?"

"It can never be like before, can it?"

"It can be better."

"Good night, darling."

"Sleep tight, Merilee."

I hung up. Lulu was watching me. "Just forget it," I snapped. "There's no chance. None. It'll never happen."

She whimpered. I told her to shut up. Then I took a bubble bath.

CHAPTER THREE

(Tape #1 with Tristam Scarr. Recorded in his chamber Nov. 19. Wears navy blue sweat suit, Air Jordan basketball sneakers, clean shave. Appears more clear-eyed than first meeting, though uneasy.)

Hoag: Ready?

Scarr: Ready, steady, go, mate.

Hoag: From the beginning, if we may.

Scarr: The beginning. Very well. I was born one evening in . . . '56, it was. Supposed to be doing m'studies in m'room. Wasn't. See, Rory's brother, Bob, who was stationed in Bremen, had told us about this station you could get on the wireless called Radio Luxembourg. They played rock 'n' roll music, which the BBC didn't back then. A fabulous moment, mate. Door closed. Turning the dial. Searching. Seeking. Hearing nothing but static. And then, very faintly . . . *it.*

Hoag: It?

Scarr: "Heartbreak Hotel." Elvis. It was nasty and hot. It was me. I freaked. From that moment on, I knew what I wanted to be, y'know?

Hoag: Yes, I do. I had a similar experience the first time I picked up *Mad* magazine. I like that anecdote. It's private, and has feeling. But can we go back to the *very* beginning?

Scarr: Wee laddie days? *(pause)* Very well. I was an only child. Born April 10, 1944.

Hoag: In?

Scarr: Rubble. Officially, it was called London. The war was still on then, of course. Mum was a nurse. Dad was a bombardier in the RAF. Dropped bombs. Poof. Martin and Meta. Named me Tristam after his grandfather. I think they met at a service dance. Neither of them was very young at the time. Or happy. They're both dead now. Bought 'em a house in Brighton to retire at. It was the only place they ever lived at was their own. He was a short geezer. Hairs sticking out of his nose and ears. Sold things door to door, or tried to. Eight-in-one kitchen implements. Miracle bloody cleaners. M'dad was accustomed to having doors slammed in his face all day long. He never complained. Just kept dreaming. He always believed the big pot of gold was just down the road.

Hoag: He wasn't wrong—he was only off by one generation.

Scarr: You got that right. Mum, she became a practical nurse. Strong woman. Very good posture. Liked everything clean, especially her little Tristam. Wore his proper school uniform, he did. Starched white shirt. Black blazer. Gray short pants. Tie. Gap. My very first act of rebellion was to be dirty . . . She saw to old ladies who were dying, and was always telling Dad about it at the table. "She's got blood in her stool again, Martin. Blood in her stool. . . ."

Hoag: You were raised in. . . ?

Scarr: A bunch of nothing London suburbs. Acton, then Ealing, then Twickenham, Teddington, Kingston . . . We were always moving.

Hoag: Wait. Time out. I thought you grew up in Liverpool.

Scarr: No. Never.

Hoag: But everything I've ever read about you said—

Scarr: All made up. They made up a lot.

Hoag: You mean the record company?

Scarr: And our manager, Marco Bartucci—the man who made us Us. Liverpool was hot. Kids from greater London weren't. So they gave us fake biographies. Christ, they said Puppy's dad was a merchant seaman from Dingle, the Liverpool docks. He was actually in jail in Louisiana for killing a man.

Hoag: And your Liverpool accent?

Scarr: The scouse was put on, like a costume. Show business.

Hoag: It certainly is. You were saying you moved around a lot.

Scarr: Mum would ask the neighborhood shopkeepers to put it on the slate. Then, when they'd get touchy about money, we'd move on to another furnished flat somewhere. "Someday, Tristam," m'dad would say, "I want you to be a *professional* man. A man in a proper chalk-striped suit and bowler who rides the train into the City every morning with the *Times* under his arm. Yessir."

Hoag: Did you want that?

Scarr: Not if he did, mate.

Hoag: You didn't get along?

Scarr: It wasn't as if we ever had a go at one another. He never had goes with anybody. Over anything. Too weak. Too afraid. He just quietly took it up the bumhole. I hated that about him. It was as if he was spending his whole life getting ready to die. Only thing he succeeded at.

Hoag: What kind of boy were you?

Scarr: You mean was I a jolly little pink-cheeked laddie? The apple of Martin and Meta's eye?

Hoag: Something like that.

Scarr: It wasn't like that.

Hoag: Didn't think it was.

Scarr: I was sickly. Asthma. Pneumonia. Tonsils. Always had breathing problems. Still do. I was home in bed a lot, swallowing bad-tasting medicines, Mum nursing me like one of her old ladies. Didn't have many mates, between that and moving to the different schools. I remember I did a lot of jigsaw puzzles. Picadilly Circus. The Grand Canyon. Diamond Fucking Head. And I spun these fairy tales in m'head—that I was a pirate king or an Indian fighter. Someone brave and strong, with mates . . . Mostly, I remember silence. The wallpaper was blue.

Hoag: You know, I've never met a celebrity who had a happy childhood.

Scarr: Nobody has a happy childhood. We just happen to get asked about ours, is all.

Hoag: Did you do well in school?

Scarr: Not very. Missed too much. Wasn't very bright either. *(laughs)* I showed no evidence of any talent of any kind as a boy. Except for m'ears. I can wiggle them. Very few people can.

Hoag: You can wiggle? I can, too. All of the Hoag men can. Let's see . . . *(silence)* Pretty decent. But can you wiggle one ear at a time?

Scarr: Impossible. No one can.

Hoag: I can.

Scarr: Balls. *(silence)* You're not really doing it.

Hoag: I am, too.

Scarr: Yes, well, as I said—I was not a good student. Somehow, I did manage to pass m'eleven-plus exams and move on up. We were living in Teddington then, I was sent to Hampton Grammar. Some pretty posh people sent their teenies there. A good crowd for young Tristam to meet on his road to becoming a professional man. Only, I fell in with the wrong crowd.

Hoag: By the wrong crowd you mean Rory?

Scarr: I do, mate.

Hoag: Can you remember the first time you two met?

Scarr: (laughs) It was in '56. I was twelve. I knew of him, of course, because he got himself in so many scrapes. A blond bloke, with a big chest and unusually short legs. Self-conscious about that, he was. To the day he died he was sensitive about his height. He was a cockney, a hard nut—quick with his mouth and his fists. The other boys were afraid of him. He was already a bit of a ted. Wore these heavy black shoes and smoked ciggies and didn't show up for classes. One day he comes up to me in the corridor and takes m'fountain pen out of m'shirt pocket and doesn't give it back. I says, "Let's have m'pen." He says, "Piss off." I says, "*You* piss off." He says, "You're a skinny little cunt, aren't you." I says, "It's m'mum's pen—she'll have m'hide if I lose it." He says, "Then she's a cunt as well." The other lads are listening by now. I'm sort of on the spot, I am. If I let him keep the pen then I've got no bloody social standing from that day forward. So we had a proper punch-up.

Hoag: Who won?

Scarr: He did. Bloodied m'nose. Tore m'shirt.

Hoag: But he gave you the pen back.

Scarr: No, he kept the pen. But he did decide I was a mate. Next morning he says to me, "I'm gonna smoke me a fag in class today." I says, "Go on." He says, "Watch me." And he did it—lit up a bleeding Woodbine right there in the middle of class. Teacher couldn't fucking believe it. Got himself royally caned for that, Rory did. But he just didn't care. They couldn't teach him anything and they couldn't hurt him. He figured as how he was smarter than all of them.

Hoag: Was he?

Scarr: Rory? He was just bloody contrary's what he was.

Different. Crazy. Still, I reckoned as how he was onto something.

Hoag: What was it?

Scarr: Being alive. *(pause)* His dad was a big, tough bloke. Had his own roofing business. He and Rory fought all the time. "Mr. Law" he called his dad, with a sneer. Quick with the belt, the old bugger was—especially after a few pints. Rory's older brother, Bob, usually got it, only he was away in the RAF at that time, so Mr. Law went after Rory.

Hoag: You and Rory became friends.

Scarr: Mates, right off. There was this, I don't know, righteous energy between us. We sparked off of each other. Did things together we'd not dream of doing on our own.

Hoag: Such as?

Scarr: Such as . . . Christ, what didn't we do? Started trash fires inside of stores. Threw rocks at nuns and cripples. Ran in front of cars in the street to make 'em hit the brakes. One time we grabbed a neighbor's cat and stuck a firecracker up its arse and lit it to see what would happen.

Hoag: And what happened?

Scarr: (laughs) They may have nine lives but they only got but one arsehole.

Hoag: That's absolutely disgusting.

Scarr: Isn't it? I'd never been happier. Even started getting a bit of a rep in the neighborhood for being a scruff. M'dad decided to have it out with me about it. Says to me, very serious, "You're being a bad boy, Tristam. Your schoolwork is inadequate. Your behavior and language are unacceptable. You'll never be a proper gentleman at this rate, just a lout. I want you to stop seeing this Rory Law."

Hoag: And what did you say?

Scarr: "Make me."

Hoag: And what did he say?

Scarr: Not a thing. I won. *(pause)* Show me that ear thing of yours again, would you, Hogarth?

(end tape)

(Tape #2 with Tristam Scarr. Recorded in his chamber Nov. 20. Appears subdued. Wears only a tweed overcoat, long Johns. Hair is in a ponytail.)

Hoag: You look tired tonight, Tristam.

Scarr: I was practicing. Haven't been to bed yet.

Hoag: Taking up a new instrument?

Scarr: No, it's that ear thing of yours. I don't get it, mate. "What's the trick?

Hoag: There's no trick. Either your ears can move independently of each other or they can't.

Scarr: Show it to me again. *(silence)* Bloody hell!

Hoag: Let's talk about when you heard Elvis sing "Heartbreak Hotel" on the radio that first time. You wanted to sound like him, look like him, *be* him. . . ?

Scarr: Me and Rory both. We were ripe for it, y'know? Something new. Something that our parents and teachers wouldn't approve of. Something that was ours. Rock 'n' roll music, it simply didn't exist here in '56. We had Tommy Steele and Johnny Gentle and vanilla pop like that. But we had no one like Elvis. No records. No radio. Nothing. Just the American movies.

Hoag: What movies?

Scarr: We were just knocked out by *The Wild One* with Marlon Brando. The motorcycles. The black leather jackets. The way the adults were so freaked out by him. The *attitude.*

It was like he was saying, "Fuck all of you," y'know? I'll never forget this one conversation. Somebody says to him "What are you rebelling against?" And Brando, he says, "Whattaya got?" *(laughs)* Whattaya fucking got! We couldn't get over that. James Dean in *Rebel Without a Cause.* That was another movie we freaked for. And *Blackboard Jungle*, with all of these wonderfully scruff students who hated Glenn Ford's bleedin' guts. The theme song to that was "Rock Around the Clock," sung by Bill Haley and the Comets. Me and Rory we ate those movies up. Saw 'em over and over again. America, it seemed like some kind of paradise to us over here then. It was Technicolor. We were black and white. It was Marilyn Monroe. We were Dame May Whitty. You blokes over there had your own bleedin' cars to take your dolly birds for rides in. Our parents couldn't afford cars here, mate. America, it was the land of the free.

Hoag: Wait, wait: "What's that I see/From across the sea?/The land of the free/More for me/Over there, the sky/It don't ever get gray/Ain't no one to tell ya/What not to say/More for me."

Scarr: You were a regular bleedin' little rocker, weren't you? Wouldn't know it to look at you now.

Hoag: Good breeding prevails in the end.

Scarr: Don't wager on it, Hogarth. Where was I? . . . Ah yes, once we got into Radio Luxembourg, we got turned on to a lot of the American rock 'n' roll music—Jerry Lee Lewis, Eddie Cochran, Buddy Holly, Ricky Nelson. Blew our minds. All of it. It was definitely where we wanted to be.

Hoag: What about skiffle? Wasn't that an important influence on early groups like Us?

Scarr: Skiffle was a craze, and it *was* ours—kind of a cross between washboard folk and trad jazz. Got started by the song "Rock Island Line" by Lonnie Donegan, who played in Chris Barber's jazz band. A skiffle band had two guitars, a banjo, washboard and upright bass. Three chords. Four/four beat. Very basic like, y'know? But it was *there.* We could hear Elvis and Bill Haley in it. And we could *do* it. All we needed was a 78 of "Hock Island Line," which cost six shillings, and a guitar. And we didn't necessarily have to play it that well. Guitar was entirely different back then. Wasn't the top-gun lead thing it became after Clapton and Page came along. Back then it was more of a rhythm instrument, like a ukulele. The saxophone was the lead instrument. Ricky Nelson had a guitarist who could bend a note, James Burton. And Cliff Richard, who I reckon you could call the first genuine British rock 'n' roll star, he had a fellow called Hank Marvin who could play.

Hoag: You and Rory decided you wanted to play.

Scarr: Rory, he got his mum to give him one for Christmas. I sent away for mine, a Spanish acoustic with wire strings that made m'fingers bleed. Came with an instruction book, *Guitar Made Easy*, by this geezer with glasses called Johnny Baughan.

Hoag: You wrote a song about him, too.

Scarr: Yes. "For Johnny Baughan." He was m'first and only music teacher. The book was mostly about how to play folk songs, but it did have these diagrams in the back showing where to put the fingers to make this or that chord. So we got our guitars, Rory and me, and we set about learning 'em. After school. Instead of school. At m'flat, since nobody was around during the day, and we had a phonograph. We smoked Woodies and played the 78 of "Rock Island Line" over and over and tried to imitate how it sounded. It could be done, y'see. So could the look, the Elvis look. The look was perhaps even more important. Creased ducks-arse hair with sidies—that's sideburns, to you. Drainies . . .

Hoag: Drainies?

Scarr: Drainpipes, which is what your jeans looked like since they were so bleeding tight. Only way to get 'em that tight was to wear 'em in the bath with you, the water as hot as you could stand it. M'dad figured as how I was daft. Looked in on me once in there and said "Mrs. Scarr, your son Tristam is taking a bath with his new trousers on, he is. Moaning, he is."

Hoag: Moaning?

Scarr: Bath was also where I learned to sing. The echo, y'know. At first I tried to imitate Elvis. Then it was Little Richard.

Hoag: Why him?

Scarr: My voice wasn't deep enough to do a really proper Elvis.

Hoag: That sandpapery quality your voice has—was that how you sounded from the start?

Scarr: Christ, no. That took years of Woodbines and whiskey and screaming into shitty microphones.

Hoag: What did you sound like back then, in the tub?

Scarr: Like any other lad, I expect. Bad. Actually, I've never had a great voice, mate. Or even a good one. It's *effective*.

Hoag: Aren't you being a little modest?

Scarr: I'm being honest, like you asked. I mean, Rod Stewart isn't Placido Fucking Domingo either, y'know?

Hoag: How did you end up being the singer?

Scarr: Rory didn't like doing it. Thought it was too feminine.

Hoag: You were telling me about the look.

Scarr: Right. Pointy black shoes—winklepickers we called 'em. Black leather jacket. Pink shirt and socks.

Hoag: Sounds like a swell outfit.

Scarr: Oh, we were bleedin' swells, all right, with our Spanish acoustics, spots on our faces, twelve, thirteen years old. Double trouble, we were.

Hoag: What did Martin and Meta think of all of this?

Scarr: They'd always figured as how I'd never amount to anything, and this here was proof of it.

Hoag: What about the others at school? What did they think of you?

Scarr: That we were teds. The surprise was the dollies. For the first time, they started taking notice of us two scruffs at the chip shops. Partly because they knew Mum and Dad wouldn't want 'em to. Partly because our trousers were so bloody tight. *(laughs)*

Hoag: You mentioned Little Richard. He was an important influence?

Scarr: I told you about Rory's brother Bob being away in Bremen. When he finished his conscript and came home we were telling him how much we loved Elvis and Bill Haley, and he said if that's the case then it's time you hear the *real* thing. He said Bill Haley didn't invent "Shake, Rattle and Roll"—Joe Turner did. And he pulled out a bleedin' trunk full of records he'd bought over there by black performers we'd never heard of—Little Richard, Chuck Berry, Fats Domino, James Brown, Elmore James, Jimmy Reed, Muddy Waters—on labels like Chess of Chicago, and Sun of Memphis. Rhythm and blues, Hogarth. A lot of the rock 'n' roll music we'd been into was nothing more than a cleaned-up white version of R and B, which was much nastier than Elvis. We freaked out over it, of course. Wore out Bob's records. Went into London looking for more in the jazz shops on Charing Cross Road. Found some used ones—Otis Spann, Bo Diddley, T-Bone Walker . . .

Hoag: Was anyone else listening to R and B here?

Scarr: Mate, nobody here had ever *heard* of it. Except for a handful of us. There were a few other blokes at school playing skiffle, forming groups. It was when Rory and me were fourteen that we decided it was time to start a group of our own.

(end tape)

* * *

(Tape #3 with Tristam Scarr. Recorded in his chamber Nov. 21. Wears flannel shirt and faded denim overalls. Seems especially anxious to talk.)

Scarr: There's something I neglected to mention before. About myself. You should know about it.

Hoag: Yes?

Scarr: I can raise one of m'eyebrows. *(silence)* See?

Hoag: How about the other eyebrow?

Scarr: Other eyebrow?

Hoag: Can you raise it, too? On its own, I mean.

Scarr: No, that one doesn't move. *(pause)* Are you saying you can raise *either* eyebrow? *(silence)* Bloody hell!

Hoag: You decided to form a rock 'n' roll band. How come?

Scarr: To meet dolly birds.

Hoag: That was the only reason?

Scarr: That was plenty. First thing we did, right off, was work on a name. Had to have a name, didn't we?

Hoag: You know, I keep finding myself surprised when you and Rory sound like a couple of kids. But you *were* kids.

Scarr: That we were. We talked it over real serious like. Came up with a number of possibilities—The Desperados, The Rebels, The Rattlers, The Rock Men, The Rough Boys. That's what we settled on—The Rough Boys. Sounded, I don't know . . .

Hoag: Rough?

Scarr: That's it. Now that we had a name we had to have some proper electric guitars. Our acoustics just wouldn't do, not for rock 'n' rolling. We begged our mums and dads for the money to buy 'em, but they said no—Rory was about to get thrown out of Hampton, and I wasn't doing much better. To them, rock 'n' roll music was partly to blame. It *was* all we did.

Hoag: So where did you get the money?

Scarr: (pause) From the cash drawer of a fish-and-chips shop.

Hoag: You're kidding.

Scarr: This old geezer, Murray, ran this little neighborhood shop near my flat. A trusting sort, he was—used to turn his back to the money drawer when he was working the fryer. The *open* money drawer. It wasn't as if we planned it. We were just in there ordering chips one day, talking things over, and we saw this money sitting right there, and bam, that electricity I told you of passed between us. The geezer never knew what hit him.

Hoag: I don't suppose you paid him back when you hit it big?

Scarr: Make a nice story, wouldn't it? With interest, and perhaps a blanket to keep him snug in his old age? Fact is, it wasn't so much as a consideration. Fuck the bugger. Never claimed I was an angel. Don't try to make me out one. We took the money straight to Bell Music in Ewell Road, Surrey. They had gorgeous equipment there. It was a trip just to hold it. Made me feel like Chuck Berry. We had just enough for a pair of hollow-body Hoffman Senators and two old secondhand Vox fifteen-watt amps. Took 'em home, plugged 'em in, ran our fingers over the strings, and it was incredible. The sound reverberated. It was *alive.*

Hoag: Did you and Rory have any sense of your individual talents this early on?

Scarr: Hmm . . . good question.

Hoag: I try.

Scarr: Rory had a knack. He would toy with a progression of chords, and have it come out sounding like something. He could *invent.* Me, I was the one ready to stick m'bleedin' neck out. Comes time for the vocalizing, for showing some personality, a lot of the blokes faded to the back of the stage with their guitars. Not me. I wanted the mike. I wanted people paying attention to me, thinking I was special.

Hoag: You still say you were doing all of this just to meet girls?

Scarr: Don't get deep on me, Hogarth . . . Of course, I also had poetry inside me, though I didn't know that yet. There were plenty of unknown R and B songs around for us to play. Didn't need to write our own for years.

Hoag: You mentioned there were other guys at school forming groups.

Scarr: Scruffs and misfits, all of 'em. Jim McCarty and Paul Samwell-Smith were at Hampton. They ended up forming the Yardbirds with Chris Dreja, Keith Relf, and Top Topham. Then Top left and Eric Clapton took his place. I got to know Eric and Keith a couple of years later when we were at Kingston Art College together.

Hoag: I never knew you went to college.

Scarr: Not college—*art* college. Every bleedin' rocker in the U.K. went to art college, Hogarth, except for Michael Jagger, who went to the London bleedin' School of Economics. Lennon went to one. Keith Richard, Townshend, Ray Davies of the Kinks, Eric, Pagey, Ron Wood, John Mayall . . . Know the old saying about how whores turn to religion when they get old? Rockers turn to painting. Art college is why. Art college and acid. *(laughs)* It was where they stuck us if we were dim and contrary and weren't in prison yet. I reckon they thought we'd be pacified by playin' with the finger paints. It was all a goof. Plenty of free time. Plenty of dollies in black stockings going through their artistic phase, if you know what that means. The only one who actually took it serious was Townshend, who to this day thinks he's not so much a rocker as a bleedin' concept artist, whatever the fuck that is . . . Where were we? . . . Yes, there were a few other blokes at Hampton playing. And we needed one to play bass—Derek. Rory and I both knew him, though not well. He sang in the choir. Was very popular. Good-looking. Nice clothes and manners. The sort that even the loveliest dolly birds wanted to stroke on the head. Christ, the *teachers* loved him. He had a few bob—dad was a dentist. Underneath, though, Derek was really a scruff, very into the Everly Brothers and Duane Eddy. Got a girl preggers when he was fourteen.

Hoag: Is that so? What happened?

Scarr: She had the baby, I believe. Of course, it was all hushed up good and proper when we hit it big. You'll have to ask Derek about it. I'm sure he'll recall—it isn't as if he's come in through the front door much since then, has he?

Hoag: He had a guitar?

Scarr: A Watkins Rapier. When we told him we wanted to have him in the Rough Boys to play bass and sing harmony with me, he said, "No problem." That's what he said to just about everything through the years—"No problem." An agreeable bloke. Any group that stays together has to have one or two like him, with all the madness around . . . We took his Rapier to Bell Music and had it restrung as a bass. Derek kicked in for a microphone for us to sing into. *(laughs)* You know how on stage he always came over and sang his harmony into my mike, standing there face to face with me?

Hoag: One of your trademarks. Sure.

Scarr: That came about because one mike was all we could afford that day at Bell Music.

Hoag: How did you three sound?

Scarr: Awful. Derek didn't know how to play the bass. But he picked it up soon enough. And he had that sweet, high-pitched voice that sounded good against mine, especially as mine got rougher. What we needed then, of course, was a drummer, and that got to be something of a hassle—very few blokes knew how to play the drums, and those who did didn't know how to play rock 'n' roll. Derek found us our first one, Andy Clarke, who played them in the school band. The four of us sounded bloody awful together. After a while, we finally figured out it was Andy, so out he went. And we were back to having no drummer. Then Rory got the boot from Hampton, which meant he had to work for Mr. Law in the roofing business.

Hoag: He didn't get along with his dad.

Scarr: Or with heights. Also meant we had to practice nights now, only that's when everybody's mums and dads were home. So we had no place to play. That was the first time we broke up. First of many.

Hoag: What you needed was a drummer whose parents both worked nights.

Scarr: Did better than that, actually. One day on the job Rory met this bricklayer called Jackie Horner who said he'd played drums in a trad jazz band and had a hankering to try rock 'n' roll. Couple of years older than us, he was. Had an uncle who ran a lorry repair garage, and he said we could use the garage to practice in at night. A fucking dream, this was. Could play as loud as we wanted, as late as we wanted. Even nick a tow van for gigs, once we started getting 'em . . . Christ, haven't thought about those nights in the garage in a long time. It was so wonderfully scruff there. Freezing cold, smelling of oil. We'd play half the night, eating chips, drinking beer, smoking Woodies. Whatever dolly Derek was seeing would come by for a listen and bring her dolly friends. Was a big thing for 'em, hanging around late at night in this unheated garage with greasy rock 'n' rollers. Naughty, y'know? They were our first groupies. Wonder where they are now . . . What was that one's name . . . Molly? Yes. She and I'd get it on in the back of a lorry with a blanket around us. She wanted to be a beautician, as I remember. Can't remember her face.

Hoag: How did you guys sound?

Scarr: Like a band now. Jackie's drumming pulled the different pieces together, gave Derek's bass a proper beat to hold onto. This was terrific progress for us. Meant they could dance to us now.

Hoag: What was your repertoire?

Scarr: Our "repertoire"? *(laughs)* The basics—"Blue Suede Shoes," "Jailhouse Rock," "That'll Be the Day," "Maybelline" . . .

Hong: Tell me about your first gig.

Scarr: This dolly who was hot for Derek convinced her rich dad to have the Rough Boys play at her graduation party. Rory and me, we didn't even know how much to charge. Jackie thought ten pounds was fair, so that was our price—in advance, so we could buy our outfits. We all wore black trousers, white shirts and red ties. It wasn't until we pulled up in our town van at this posh house, and saw all of these posh kids going in, that it hit us that we'd never played in front of an audience before. At least not an audience of more than four appreciative dollies. Must have been fifty laddies and dollies, and some mums and dads as well. Staring right at us.

Hoag: At Woodstock you played in front of half a million.

Scarr: We froze—all of us except for Jackie. Hands shook so bad we couldn't set up our gear. Jackie had to calm us down, light us a Woodie. A solid soul he was. On our first number, "Maybelline," m'voice cracked. But after I worked up a proper sweat I was fine. We were fine. They danced. They clapped. Had a grand old time. So did we. Christ, it was a gas up there, being the life of the party. *The life*—that was the best part of it for me, I think . . . From there we started playing youth club dances, church halls, picnics, here and there.

Hoag: Looking back, did you have any idea where this was going to lead you?

Scarr: None, other than to get us laid—and in punch-ups.

Hoag: Punch-ups?

Scarr: The dollies would give us the eye. I'd have 'em up on stage. Give 'em a big kiss, tell 'em their boyfriends were ugly. The boyfriends didn't much fancy that. More often than not they'd be waiting for us out in the parking lot. A rocker had to be able to give it back in the early days. Rory and me and Jackie gave it back good. Derek always hid in the van—afraid for his face he was. It actually didn't occur to us then that the Rough Boys might be a ticket for us, Hogarth. We thought about today. Having a laugh. Having it off. We didn't think much about tomorrow. Didn't seem to be any point in that. Wasn't as if any of our lot were going anywhere, were we?

Hoag: When did your thinking change?

Scarr: Not long after that. I remember the date distinctly—October of '62. That's when the Beatles released "Love Me Do." Things just exploded here after that. If you happened to be in a group like ours, you started thinking maybe it'll happen to us, too. Maybe we'll be the next ones. Why not, y'know? Within two years we were big. Very big. A bloody shame that Jackie couldn't be part of it. He was the one who had to go when Puppy joined the group. Marco's doing. Bloody shame, what with Jackie being so important to us early on.

Hoag: I suppose every famous band has its Pete Best, the poor slob who missed the boat. Whatever happened to him?

Scarr: He's Jack, mate. M'chauffeur.

(end tape)

CHAPTER FOUR

I'd been living at Gadpole a week before I realized someone else was living there, too. Like I said, the place wasn't small. I had dressed early for Merilee's opening and was shooting pool in the panelled billiard room and snatching occasional glances at myself in the bevelled mirror behind the bar. Hard not to peek. There's only a very select handful who can appear totally at home in a tux: Fred Astaire. Cary Grant. Marlene Dietrich. Me.

"So you'll be the writer then?" asked a female voice, most English.

I turned to find a willowy black-haired girl there in the doorway. She was unusually tall and wore a sullen expression and no makeup. She didn't need makeup. Her hair was lustrous and abundant, her eyes an arresting cornflower blue, her lips fat and pouty. Her arms and legs were very long, her hands and feet man-sized. She wore a wool buffalo plaid shirt untucked over black tights and pink ballet slippers. She was very sexy, if you like them tall and sullen and certainly not yet twenty.

"That's right," I replied, going back to work on the table. I had a nice light touch that evening. "It's Hoagy."

"I'm called Violet. Pammy told me you were here. Don't you just love her?"

She seemed particularly young with her mouth open and words coming out, or maybe I was just getting to be particularly old. "Yes, I do. You're a friend of T. S.?"

"Kind of."

"Been modeling long?"

"A few months. I was just in Paris." She frowned. "How did you know I model?"

"I'm clairvoyant."

She giggled. "Is that like being gay?"

"Better. You don't have to take it up the . . . I'm sorry. I'm *very* sorry. I must be spending too much time with T. S."

"Oh, you don't have to worry about me. I've done everything." She leaned against the bar and lit a cigarette, very blasé. "And then some."

"Been around, have you?"

"Kind of."

Chances were she had been. Women who hang around with rock stars have to be game for anything, such as sex with four guys at once, or having an array of objects rammed into various personal orifices, or sitting naked in tubs full of hot fudge, or all of the above. Writers, we don't have female followers like that. Ours tend to be short, nervous copy editors named Charlotte or Rhonda who mostly want to talk about Pynchon and Coover.

"Ooh. I love your dog!"

Lulu was watching us disapprovingly from under the bar.

"She loves to be loved."

Violet smiled at me. She liked me looking at her, and I was looking at her.

"I was expecting someone old and crawly with a beard, actually," she informed me. "You're cute for a writer."

"It's true. I was voted cutest American writer of the year in '83. Joyce Carol Oates came in second."

She frowned. Modern American literature didn't seem to be one of her strengths. A point in her favor. "Would you be going into London?" she asked.

"No, I always dress like this for a quiet evening at home."

"Can I come? It's so bloody boring out here."

"I'd be happy to give you a lift in, but I do have plans."

"Oh. Forget it then—I thought we could go dancing."

I checked my grandfather's Rolex. "I'd best be off," I said, racking my cue.

"Where are you living, anyhow?"

"Second floor, west wing, guest suite. End of the—"

"Ooh, the leather room?"

"The very one."

"I'm directly down the hall in the blue room," she said. "I love leather. Especially black leather."

"Then I'm sure you and T. S. have a lot in common."

"Oh, we do."

Jack offered me my choice of the two, count 'em two, utility vehicles. These were kept apart from T. S.'s show cars in a small garage adjacent to Jack's office and rooms.

One was a dinged-up '79 Peugeot 504 diesel station wagon. The other was a gleaming twenty-year-old Austin Mini Cooper. I went for the mini.

"By the way," I said, taking the keys from him, "I should be very cross with you."

"Me, sir?"

"You didn't tell me the other day you're Jackie Horner, original drummer of the Rough Boys."

His red face got redder. "That was a long time ago, sir." He scruffed at the ground with his foot. "Boyhood stuff."

"Still, I really *am* going to interview you now."

"About?"

"Your recollections. Your feelings about what it's like to have gotten so close to it, but . . ."

"Missed it?" he demanded indignantly, puffing his chest out. "Didn't miss it. Not at all. I'm right here. Got m'health, a few bob in the bank—that's more than a lot of 'em can say, believe me."

"You're not bitter?"

He let out a short, humorless laugh. "Doesn't pay to be bitter."

"So why the words of warning the other day?"

"I have my reasons."

"What are they?"

"You're familiar with our right-hand drive?" he asked, changing the subject.

"I am."

Lulu and I climbed into the mini. It had a burled walnut dash, a small fridge and a monster stereo system. The seats were upholstered in mink. Lulu settled into hers, immensely pleased.

I rolled down my window. "Say, this isn't exactly factory issue, is it?"

"Customized by a chap in London who does Rolls work for the Arab sheiks. A little something extra under the bonnet, as well. You'll go left at the main road. In five miles you'll reach the A-Twenty-three. Follow that in."

"Thank you, Jackie."

"It's Jack, sir. Please."

"My mistake. How about that interview? I can work around your schedule."

He smiled, reached in, and straightened my bow tie for me. It didn't need straightening. "Have a good trip, sir."

The mini kicked right over. I eased her slowly down the gravel drive toward the front gate, checking out the right-hand drive and Jack in the rear-view mirror. He was watching me, hands on his hips. What was he hiding?

I found an ice-cold bottle of Dom Perignon in the little fridge, along with a chilled pewter mug. I helped myself. There was no current stuff among the tapes—only sixties soul music. No complaints here. I put on some Aretha Franklin very loud. The guards opened the front gate wide, and we were on our way.

Lady Soul was hot. The mini was hotter. I found the highway and worked my way happily through the city-bound traffic and the champagne. Lulu rode sitting up so she could take in the foreign sights out of her window and, occasionally, snuffle at them.

We reached London in time to do some vital reconnaissance for later in the evening. Then I drove us over to the West End and ditched the mini around the corner from the theater. The Haymarket is a fine old stage—intimate, well-maintained, steeped in theatrical history and tradition. There used to be a few theaters like it left on Broadway, only they tore them down a couple of years ago to make way for a hotel complex that belongs next to an airport. In Atlanta.

Merilee had reserved a pair on the aisle. I let Lulu have the aisle seat so she could see better. She whimpered softly when the lights came up on Merilee. She wasn't the only one. Merilee looked gorgeous that night, her waist-length golden hair and white dress aglow under the stage lights. Not that my ex-wife is conventionally beautiful. Her nose and chin are patrician to the point of mannish, and her forehead is much too high. Plus, she's not exactly delicately proportioned. Her shoulders are broad and sloped, her back muscular, her legs big and powerful. She was, I realized, significantly taller than Anthony Andrews. She had to wear flat shoes and slouch into her hip to stay eye to eye with him.

They played it bright and peppy, like Barry is meant to be played. Her Tracy was steely control on the outside, a dithery, vulnerable mess on the inside. It's hard to not think of Hepburn in the part—Barry did write it for her. But that night, on the Haymarket stage, Merilee made the role of Tracy Lord her own.

When it was over, Lulu and I worked our way through the opening night mob backstage to tell her. She was in her dressing room, surrounded by admirers and backers, laughing, giddy. I watched her from across the room until she spotted me. Her smile dropped. Her green eyes widened. We stared at each other for what seemed like hours. Then I smiled, and she smiled. And the other people in the room and the years and the bad times melted away.

"How was I?" she asked, accepting the dozen long-stemmed roses I'd brought her.

"It wasn't the worst thing you've ever done."

"Thank you, darling."

"And you've never looked lovelier, but I suppose you already know that."

"A gal only knows it if her guy says so."

"Am I your guy?"

"Could be. I forgot how nice you look in a tux."

"Careful, my head turns easily."

She dabbed at my upper lip with her finger. "You shaved off your mustache."

"Like it?"

"It reminds me of how you looked when we met."

"I'll take that as a yes."

"I gave it as a yes."

Slowly, each of us became aware of this moaning sound originating from floor level. Lulu, ears back and tail thumping, was desperately trying to scale Mount Merilee.

"Oh, Lulu, sweetness! No, you'll tear my costume!"

Merilee bent over and held Lulu down with her hands. These Lulu nuzzled and licked, all the while circling Merilee in a frenzy.

"You'd best take her out, darling," Merilee said. "I'll change."

"Not too much," I cautioned.

She laughed. It was one of our corny old jokes from back when we were falling madly in love, and I'd meet her backstage every evening.

She emerged a half hour later dressed in a Laura Biagiotti skirt and sweater of mocha brown cashmere, a blouse of white silk and Tanino Crisci boots. There was a trench coat over her arm and a first-class Worth & Worth Statler fedora on her head. The Statler had been mine, until she convinced me it was too small for me.

She liked the mini. Lulu liked sitting in her lap.

We went to the Hungry Horse, which is on Fulham Road in what was a hip South Ken neighborhood twenty years ago. Now there seemed to be a lot of places there offering American cheeseburgers and televised NFL football games. Certainly, this was not my idea of hip, but then neither is Pee-wee Herman.

They serve old-fashioned English food at the Hungry Horse. The dining room is a few steps down, and small, and you go in the back way through the kitchen. The tables are set against little settees. I let Merilee have the settee. I sat across from her, or I should say them. Lulu went right for her lap again. She had not paid me the slightest attention since we'd met up with Merilee.

"I've missed her," said Merilee, scratching Lulu's ears.

"I see it's mutual," I noted drily.

"She reminds me of us. The good part."

"You like to be reminded?"

"From time to time." Merilee flushed slightly, looked away. "When I'm feeling as if something is missing from my life. When I'm feeling . . . ordinary."

"That's one thing you'll never be."

We ordered blood-rare roast beef, Yorkshire pudding and a bottle of Medoc. And two martinis, very dry.

"Nothing to start with?" asked the waiter.

"Just extra olives in our martinis," I replied.

He frowned. "How many would you like?"

"Bring the jar," Merilee said. "Please."

For Merilee Nash he'd gladly have tangoed with a sheep. He returned a moment later with our martinis, very dry, an ornate bowl brimming with cocktail olives, and an autograph book, which he held before her shyly. She signed it.

I held my glass up. "To a successful run."

"To *then*." She clicked my glass with hers. "The good part."

We drank.

"How are the parents?" she asked, dunking an olive in her drink and devouring it.

I come from one of those families where no one speaks to each other. Merilee they loved. "Alive, last I heard. Yours?"

Merilee comes from one of those families where everyone speaks to each other. Me they never liked. "Well."

I dunked an olive in my drink. I was about to swallow it when I saw her gazing at it longingly. She'd always insisted mine tasted better than hers. I let her have it. Then I had one of my own. "And Zack?"

She looked down into her drink. "Zack is having serious problems with his second play."

It had been several years now since Zack had made his Broadway splash. He was overdue. "What's it about?"

"Us, apparently. Him and me. It's caused him to withdraw from me. And to get churlish." She sipped her martini. "Also to drink too much."

"Say, this sounds mighty familiar."

She smiled ruefully. "Doesn't it?"

"It's so unlike you. Truly. I mean, you're such a perfect person except for this one teeny little flaw of yours."

She stiffened. "Flaw? What flaw?"

"I hate to be the one to break it to you, Merilee, but you have terrible taste in husbands."

She covered my hand with hers and looked dreamily into my eyes. "You noticed."

We tore into our food when it came. Merilee eats like a sophomore nose tackle and never gains an ounce. It drives her friends crazy. Her women friends.

"So is it over?" I asked. "You and Zack?"

"It's acrid."

"Acrid?"

"Tell me about T. S.," she said, gently but firmly steering us elsewhere. I let her do so.

"Haven't figured him out yet. He's moody. Self-centered. Cooperative, but evasive when he wants to be. A tough nut, no question."

She helped herself to some of my roast beef. "And the novel? What's it about?"

I cleared my throat. "The last couple of years."

"I see," she said, the weather on her side of the table getting noticeably chillier. "And I'll play a featured role in it?"

"I'm trying to deal with what happened."

"From your point of view."

"It's my book."

"That's right, it is," she agreed, sharply. "I'm going to write a book myself. I'll call it *I Keep Marrying Men Who Blame Me For Their Problems*."

"Not true, Merilee."

"Not fair! I do the best I can! Why do I deserve this?"

"Look, I don't blame you. But I do have to write about us. That's how I work things out. The thing that drove us apart was I *couldn't* write."

"All of which makes it okay—even if I get trashed in print."

"You won't get trashed."

"But I will get undressed!"

"If you insist. Shall I blindfold the waiter?"

"Not funny," she snapped, glaring at me.

Lulu shifted restlessly in Merilee's lap and looked from Merilee to me, then from me to Merilee.

"It appears," I said, "as if this isn't going to work out very well. I suppose it was unrealistic to expect it would." I looked around for our waiter.

"No," she said, placing her knife and fork down on her plate. "Wait, Hoagy. Let's not do this, okay? Let's not talk about the past, the future, any of it. Can't we just enjoy now? Enjoy each other?"

I got lost in her green eyes for a second. "We can sure try."

"Good. But first I have something very serious to ask you."

"Yes, Merilee?"

"What are we having for dessert?"

We had a positively immoral concoction of cake topped with whipped fresh cream, and finished it off with coffee and port.

Then we walked, Merilee's hand on my arm, her gait as long and loping as my own. Lulu ambled happily a few feet ahead of us, so busy showing us off to the passersby that she didn't notice we were being followed. Nor did Merilee. I wasn't absolutely sure myself—I'm not exactly what you'd call an expert on trench-coat surveillance—but I swore I sensed somebody walking a careful half block or so behind us, staying stride for stride with us, measuring us.

"Hoagy, are we one of those awful couples who can't get along together but can't get along apart either?"

That one caught me flat-footed—pleasantly so. I hadn't known we were anything to her anymore, except dead.

"We've never not gotten along in London," I pointed out.

"That's right," she exclaimed, squeezing my arm. "Get me drunk?"

"With pleasure."

She thought we'd be pulling in at the Anglesea, a fine old pub on Selwood Terrace with rough wooden floors and Ruddle's on tap. We'd had fun there on our honeymoon. But I steered us past it to a fairly undistinguished looking family pub on Old Brompton Road.

It was crowded and smoky in there, and it smelled of beer and fried fish. The working-class clientele gave us the eye as we worked our way through them toward the bar—me for the tux, Merilee for being Merilee. I ordered pints of heavy Guinness draft for us and a piece of finnan haddie for Lulu. The meaty Hungry Horse menu hadn't much appealed to her. When our mugs were set before us we clinked them and drank deeply. Merilee then swiped delicately at the creamy foam on her upper lip and made a little noise akin to a discreet hiccough. Among her many gifts she happens to possess the world's most elegant belch.

The barman treated us to our second round in exchange for an autograph, which Merilee happily signed. As she handed the prized napkin back to him, she pointed to a sign prominently displayed over the bar.

"Tell me," she said, "why is tonight called Poultry Night?"

The barman flushed with embarrassment. "Well, miss, it's because . . . uh . . ."

"Because?" she pressed.

"Every woman . . . she gets a free . . ."

Merilee yelped.

". . . goose."

"Splendid custom," I declared, raising my mug to the quick-fingered drinkers behind us, as well as glancing about for a familiar face, or a shifty-eyed face, or for anyone who looked like he didn't want me to spot him. No one.

Three pale, knobby-knuckled workmen at the end of the bar bought us our third round. We returned the favor. Then I decided it was time to test those tapping feet.

"Shall we?" I asked, indicating the two square feet of vacant floor beside the jukebox.

"I thought you'd never ask, darling."

I made my song selection and gathered her in my arms. A little shudder went through her when Ray Charles's version of "Georgia on My Mind" came on. It was our song—the one we danced to over and over again that first night, at a Polish seaman's club on First Avenue and Ninth Street, where we drank up peppery vodka and each other, and then went home and didn't leave the bed for six weeks.

She was gazing at me now, her eyes brimming. "How did you know they had it?"

"Easy—I checked out every jukebox within a ten-block radius."

"You romantic fool."

"You got that half right."

"Which half?"

"Ssh."

We swayed slowly, cheek to cheek. She smelled of Crabtree and Evelyn avocado oil soap. Her smell. Also her secret—she won't tell anyone she bathes in it for fear a beauty magazine will reveal it and she'll end up smelling like every other woman in America.

When it was over Nat Cole sang us "Don't Get Around Much Anymore." Joe Williams did "In the Evening," Mel Torme "Blue and Sentimental." It was an uncommon juke.

"I don't mean to be indelicate, darling," Merilee murmured in my ear, "but are you rising to the occasion these days?"

"Try me."

She sighed. "I have."

"Try me again."

"I'm not so sure."

"Then why did you bring it up? So to speak."

Her green eyes twinkled. "A gal just likes to know these things."

We pulled up at her place on Cromwell Road a little after three. It was hidden from the road. To get there we turned in at a driveway, then passed under an archway, jogged around and found ourselves in a wonderfully private little cobbled mews of precious dolls' houses. Hers was a cheery blue number with flowers growing in the window boxes. If she had mice they were doubtless singing ones.

Our tail followed us in, then backed out onto Cromwell Road when he saw we were staying. He was in a taxicab now. Picked us up the second we left the pub.

We sat there not talking for a while with the engine running and Lulu asleep in her lap.

I broke the silence. "Going to invite us in?"

She didn't answer me right away. When she did she said, "No, I'm not."

"Okay."

"That's it? You're not going to argue with me? Paw me? Pant?"

"Too old."

She took a deep breath and let it out slowly. "It isn't simple, darling. There's Zack . . ."

"I know."

"There's also the fact that you and I failed once before, and there's no reason to believe we'll do any differently now. I don't want to live through the same pain all over again. I'm too old, too."

"I don't come with a warranty," I said. "I'm not a Hyundai Excel."

"And I'm not Donna Reed."

"Neither was Donna Reed."

"Good night, darling."

"Sleep tight, Merilee."

She woke Lulu up, kissed her on top of the head and got out. I watched her go inside of her house. So did Lulu, who scratched at the window and whimpered. I told her to shut up.

The taxi was still there, double-parked on Cromwell Road about a hundred feet from the driveway, lights on, engine running. Waiting. There were two people inside of it. One was the driver. I couldn't tell if the person in back was a man or a woman. Didn't know what he or she wanted. Sure as hell didn't feel like finding out just now, either.

I floored it. Took the first right turn on two wheels, then took a left, then a right. I kept checking the rearview mirror but I really didn't need to. I'd lost the taxi in two blocks. No way it could stay with the souped-up mini. By the time I reached the A-23 I was the only one on the road. Just me and the fog.

It was the eleventh consecutive gloomy day since I'd arrived in England, and it suited me just fine.

A click woke me.

It was the sound of the door to my suite being closed. From the inside. The floor creaked in the sitting room. Someone was moving around in there in the darkness. Lulu growled softly from her perch atop my head. I muzzled her.

A match was struck. I could see its wavering yellow glow through the open bedroom door. And hear a shuffling sound—the papers on my desk were being examined. The match went out. More footsteps in the darkness. Closer. Lulu tensed. Another match was struck. The things on my dressing table were being pored over now—the contents of my wallet, my money clip.

I turned on my bedside lamp. "Can I help?"

Violet stood at my dressing table. She wore a black Chicago Bears T-shirt and absolutely nothing else. Her breasts strained against the T-shirt.

"A match," she said, with admirable calm. She showed me the unlit cigarette that was between her fingers. In her other hand was a book of matches. "I was looking for a match, you see. Couldn't find one anywhere. Very sorry if I woke you."

"That's okay. Only, you didn't find those matches in here. I don't smoke."

"They were over by the fireplace."

"And you're not," I pointed out.

"I wasn't stealing!"

"I didn't say you were. Want to tell me what you were doing in my things?"

She lit her cigarette, came over to the bed and sat down on the edge of it. Lulu sniffed disagreeably at her, jumped down and waddled into the sitting room.

"I don't think she likes me," Violet said, watching her go.

"Nothing personal. She just gets possessive."

"I couldn't sleep, y'know? And I was a bit curious about you."

I smiled. "Okay."

"May I have a drink?"

"Help yourself."

"You?"

"Had plenty tonight, thanks."

I watched her pad into the sitting room in her non-decent T-shirt. I watched her come back, too, stirring a whiskey and soda with her index finger, which she sucked on when she was finished using it. She sat back down on the bed and took a sip of her drink. She took another sip. Then she leaned back on her elbows, crossed her bare, impossibly long legs and admired her naked foot. It was a lovely foot, slender and high-arched. She began to swing it up and down, up and . . .

"What would you like to know about me?" I asked.

"Whether you like me," she replied, looking me straight in the eye.

"You're right out of my moistest fantasies. Such as they are."

She tasted the whiskey on her lips with the tip of her tongue. "I could get in there with you."

"Are you always this shy?"

"Tris wouldn't mind y'know. Really."

"I'm married," I said. "Somewhat."

"Oh." She shrugged. "We wouldn't have to do anything, actually, except sleep. It's so much nicer sleeping with someone else, isn't it?"

She wasn't wrong. Or difficult or demanding. Or Merilee. Always, it came back to Merilee.

"Thanks, anyway. Why don't you sleep with Tris? He should be turning in soon—it's nearly dawn."

Her eyes widened. "There's a naughty name for that, isn't there?"

"Statutory rape?"

"Incest, silly. You did know he's m'daddy, didn't you?"

CHAPTER FIVE

(Tape #4 with Tristam Scarr. Recorded in his chamber Nov. 24. Wears same clothes as three days before. Does not appear to have bathed, shaved or slept since then. Room is considerably darker than before. Has turned off several lamps. Wears dark glasses.)

Hoag: I met your daughter, Violet. She's lovely.

Scarr: Careful of her, mate.

Hoag: Oh?

Scarr: She likes to nick things. What they call a . . . a . . .

Hoag: Thief?

Scarr: Kleptomaniac. Don't doubt she's a nymphomaniac as well. And an overall maniac. Just like her jolly old mum.

Hoag: Who is. . . ?

Scarr: Tulip.

Hoag: Ah. The floral motif should have been a giveaway.

Scarr: They haven't gotten along, she and Tu, since Tu found his holiness. Tries to impose her beliefs on the girl. And raises bloody hell over her things being mussed with. So I let Vi crash here, if she's into it.

Hoag: She seems very mature for her age.

Scarr: She's fifteen, if that's what you're wondering. Why, did you climb into her nickers? It's cool with me if you did. I can't exactly tell her not to do the things I did, can I? It'd be bleedin' bullshit. *(pause)* Did you?

Hoag: I've spoken with Jack a couple of times. I wouldn't exactly say he's hostile, but, well, he *is* hostile.

Scarr: He's fucking jealous is all.

Hoag: I wondered if it was something else. Something he didn't want coming out.

Scarr: Such as?

Hoag: I was hoping you'd tell me.

Scarr: I'm not tracking, Hogarth.

Hoag: The man's dead set against talking to me.

Scarr: So leave him be.

Hoag: Can't. He's too valuable a source.

Scarr: I see. I'll have a word with him then.

Hoag: Thank you. I'm interested in what the music scene was like here in '62, when the Rough Boys were first getting gigs.

Scarr: Uh-huh. There was a small R and B thing happening in and around London. Like a cult thing, really. *(pause)* Did you fuck her? It's okay, mate. I mean it.

Hoag: It didn't come up.

Scarr: (silence, then laughs) There's a good one. Bloody good.

Hoag: Now can we. . . ?

Scarr: Right. We talked about how Lonnie Donegan, of skiffle fame, had played in Chris Barber's jazz band back in the fifties. So had Alexis Korner and Cyril Davies, until they split to form Blues Incorporated, which I reckon you could call Britain's very first blues band. Charlie Watts of the Stones-to-be was on drums. Jack Bruce of Cream-to-be played bass. Blues Incorporated tried playing the trad jazz clubs around London, only the serious jazz fans—the bleedin' intellects—thought they were too scruff. So they started up their own club in a basement under a teashop in Ealing—the Ealing Club. Those of us who were into R and B took to hanging out there when we weren't playing a gig. Me and Rory, Michael Jagger, Keith, Brian, John Mayall, Long John Baldry . . . We were all mates then, before there was competition and egos and the like. We'd rap about music and gigs, and anybody could have a blow up on stage. Got up there m'self one night, roaring drunk I was, and sang "Ooh-ee Baby," the Albert King song, with Blues Incorporated. Cyril backed me up on harp. Played it like a monster. Right then I decided to learn harp m'self. *(yawns)* All of which meant the Rough Boys started sounding bluesier. We added "Please, Please, Please," a James Brown song, and "Spoonful," the Howlin' Wolf song, which Cream did years later. After Blues Incorporated split up, Cyril formed a new band, the All Stars, and they got a gig at the Island. That's Eel Pie Island, which was an old twenties dance hall out on this island in the middle of the Thames at Twickenham. Cyril put in the word for us and got us a gig there as well. There was a small blues circuit then—the Railway Hotel in Harrow, St. Mary's Parish Hall in Richmond, Studio Fifty-One in London. We played all of 'em. Met people. Talked ourselves up. Only, we kept playin' the weddings and church dances as well, which was a mistake. Couldn't get known for anything that way. I thought we should be a blues band. The Beatles were already rockin', y'know? Rory and the others, they still liked playing "Blue Suede Shoes." While we were busy arguing over it, Decca went and signed up the Stones to a recording contract. Pissed me off. *(yawns)* They were playin' at Crawdaddy then. Turnin' it into a big R and B club. We followed 'em in there after they signed with Decca. We were always followin' 'em. Played the Marquee after 'em as well. Only now—now the knock against us was we was too much like the bleedin' Stones. We sounded different, but the people makin' decisions, the record people, they went by categories. Rory fought the categories. He believed in the power of the music. *(yawns)* I . . .

Hoag: You didn't?

Scarr: Hmm? . . . Sorry . . . I was more a realist, I reckon.

Hoag: Realist?

Scarr: To me all we lacked was a proper gimmick. Or management. It's all a hustle, isn't it? You've got to get noticed, is all . . . I think I've had it for tonight, mate.

Hoag: You do look somewhat beat. I meant to tell you, Tristam—somebody was following me in London last night.

Scarr: Know that feeling. So well. Seems real, doesn't it? It's the acid . . . So real . . .

Hoag: This *was* real.

Scarr: Mmm-mmmmm . . .

Hoag: Any idea why someone would be following me? *(silence)* Tristam? *(silence)* Hello?

(end tape)

(Tape #1 with Jack Horner recorded in his office Nov. 25. There is a cluttered desk, portable heater, girlie calendar, gun rack. Contents: Browning 20-gauge over-under, Remington 1100 automatic, pre-'64 Winchester bolt action sporting rifle. Door leads into parlor of his apartment. Spartanly furnished.)

Horner: I'd like to apologize about before, sir. Didn't mean to appear rude.

Hoag: Are you still opposed to looking into the past?

Horner: I am. But I understand you have a job to do. Mr. Scarr, he made it clear to me.

Hoag: What did you mean before when you told me, "It wouldn't be bright"?

Horner: Just talk, sir.

Hoag: I thought you might have been referring to Puppy's death.

Horner: Puppy's death?

Hoag: T. S. seems to think it was no accident.

Horner: (silence) I was road manager when it happened. I knew what went on.

Hoag: And?

Horner: Pup, for all of his wildness, he knew his limits. He wouldn't have taken that much speed on his own. Someone slipped him a monster dose without him knowing it. Replaced the pills he was taking with stronger ones. At least, that's what I always figured.

Hoag: Any idea who?

Horner: Had to be one of us, didn't it?

Hoag: Did it?

Horner: It's not like they were on the road when it happened. They were recording, or trying to, at Rory's country place in the Cotswolds. I was helping with the equipment. The band was there, Tulip, Marco, a couple of ladies . . .

Hoag: You're saying you think someone in or close to the band murdered Puppy Johnson?

Horner: Who else could it have been?

Hoag: Did you tell this to the police at the time?

Horner: Yessir, I did. And there was a thorough investigation—all quite hush-hush, so the papers wouldn't get hold of it. But the pills were never found. No case was made against anyone. So it was ruled an accident.

Hoag: (pause) T. S. seems to feel you're pretty bitter about being dropped from the band. That you hated Puppy.

Horner: I told you before, I'm not a bitter man. And I don't appreciate you suggesting—

Hoag: What were your responsibilities as roadie?

Horner: I did what needed to be done.

Hoag: Did you buy Puppy's dope for him?

Horner: From time to time—when they were on the road. At home they were all on their own. I wasn't any drug dealer. I don't know where that speed came from and that's the truth. One minute they were playing in Rory's studio. Next minute Pup was dead. That's all I know.

Hoag: T. S. and I were talking last night about the club days, before the Rough Boys caught on.

Horner: That was wartime, that.

Hoag: Between the different bands?

Horner: Between T. S. and Rory. That was their way, when they were young. Arguing was how they talked. Punching was how they argued. Hot-tempered, both of 'em. Sometimes they'd go at it right there on stage. Derek and I would just look at each other and roll our eyes . . . Rory, he got in a proper punch-up with Mr. Law over his work habits as a roofer, or lack of 'em. He and T. S. took a room together, near the garage where we played. Bloody awful place it was—two bare mattresses on the floor, a single suitcase between the two of 'em, cigarette butts and beer bottles everywhere. The lights and heat were coin-operated, which meant it was always freezing and dark in there. And they were always sick. Never ate. I'd go over and they'd be wrapped in blankets on the floor in the dark, coughing, Rory strumming away on his guitar. Even slept with the thing. The Rough Boys weren't earning more than a few bob a week for the four of us. Some nights there'd only be five, six people listening to us in the clubs. I still laid bricks. Derek was a clerk at a men's clothing store. Those two, they lived the music twenty-four hours a day. They wanted to be rock 'n' roll stars, or die trying . . . The thing you should bear in mind, Mr. Hoag, is it was always T. S. and

Rory's hand. Derek and I were just along for the ride. Until . . . until it was just Derek along for the ride.

Hoag: Can we talk about that?

Horner: (pause) I suppose it goes all the way back to when we attended the Negro Blues Festival, autumn of '63 at Fairfield Hall in Croydon. Giorgio Gomelsky, who managed Crawdaddy, pulled it together. Giorgio managed the Stones until they left him for Andrew Loog Oldham. This blues festival, it was a showcase of American blues greats—Muddy Waters, Otis Spann and the one and only Mad Dog Johnson. Mad Dog was a giant, enormously fat old geezer from Louisiana. Six feet six. Weighed twenty stone easily. And admitted to being seventy years old. They called him Mad Dog for two reasons. One was he could make the mouth harp sound just exactly like a dog growling. Two was that he was stark, staring mad. This we didn't know yet. All we knew was he was the real thing. T. S., he got it into his head we should somehow hook up with him. Rory wasn't mad about the idea, but he had to admit that the Rough Boys needed a push. We approached Mad Dog backstage after his performance, where we found him with his "niece," Mabel, who was perhaps twenty and traveled with him. T. S. told him how much we dug him, and how we played the blues ourselves and would love to play with him sometime. Mad Dog just mumbled something, and then T. S. tried to shake his hand. In response, Mad Dog swatted T. S. away with the back of his hand, sent him flying against the wall. And went after him, cursing and spitting. He'd have killed T. S. if we all hadn't pried him off. Turned out he didn't like to shake hands. Turned out he drank twenty-four hours a day, ranted and raved and was violent. Carried a loaded gun as well. Still, T. S. was not to be denied. After he came to he asked this Mabel to get Mad Dog to Crawdaddy the next night. She did, and he got up there with us, this ancient black giant who didn't even know where he was half the time. It was a wild gig—him drinking whiskey from the bottle, yelling out lyrics that made no sense, doing these strange things with his harp, like flickering his Adam's apple with his fingers as he played it. But it got us noticed. Which was what T. S. was after, I think. Right off a bloke came up and said we ought to let him manage us.

Hoag: This would be Marco Bartucci?

Horner: No. Marco came later. This was a geezer named Eli Gushen, who said he was a cinema hall manager, and assured us he could get the Rough Boys, featuring Mad Dog Johnson, a gig in a package tour. Those were a big deal back then. They'd put one headliner together with an assortment of musical acts—some on the way up, some on the way down, some on the way nowhere—and they'd tour the cinema halls performing one-night stands. Eli got us a spot in a two-week tour of the north, opening for Jerry Lee Lewis. Twenty pounds a week for us all. So we hit the road. Spent our days in a motor coach, our nights in mining town railway hotels, living on eggs and chips, washing out our socks in the sink, all of us in one room except for Mad Dog and Mabel. "This is it, lads," T. S. kept saying. "We've made it." Christ, we were practically cleaning up after the elephants—Jerry Lee would not even say hello to us—but T. S., he was in heaven. And he worshiped Mad Dog. Pestered him constantly for stories about the old days. Nicked his expressions, like "Lord have mercy" and "Hoo, Lord." And that quality to his voice that he became so famous for, that rough quality, it came from imitating Mad Dog . . . He was a bit of business, was Mad Dog. There was always this ungodly whooping and hollering coming from his room. One night he shot out his hotel room window and got all of us thrown out.

Hoag: How did you go over musically?

Horner: Piss poor. At least at Crawdaddy and the other clubs around London there were a few blues followers. Not in the north. Saturday nights there they wanted to drink up a lot of ale and hear "Rock Around the Clock." We got booed for playing the blues. T. S. and Rory got into quite a row over it. The tour was basically a disaster. A rip-off as well. Eli was holding our money, see, saying we'd get it after the tour. Only we didn't—he claimed it had all gone to cover our expenses. Turned out he was a kind of pimp who got young groups like us to fill out the bill for nothing. We got our money though. Rory and me took him out back of the bus and beat the shit out of him and emptied his wallet for him. He was only worth seven pounds, so we took his coat and his shoes and sold those. T. S. thought we should give the money to Mad Dog. His work visa was up and he had no passage home to America. So we did. Not that T. S. was entirely without reasons of his own. See, he was having it off with Mabel and wanted to give her the go.

Hoag: Tired of her?

Horner: Not exactly. *(laughs)* Mad Dog wasn't the only member of the family who packed a gun, sir.

(end tape)

(Tape #1 with Derek Gregg recorded in parlor of his Georgian town house in Bedford Square, Nov. 26. Room dominated by cherry wood gun case featuring museum-grade collection of American muzzle loaders, including 1775 Maryland Committee of Safety musket with brass wrist escutcheon, A. Waters and Son 1842 smoothbore percussion musket, 1847 Sappers & Miners musketoon. Former Us bassist looks remarkably like he did twenty years before. Sandy hair still cut in moppet style. Few if any lines on face or neck. No suggestion of paunch under

black silk shirt. Jeans and boots are also black. Companion is a muscular swarthy young man in matching attire. Gregg asks him to leave us. He does so, sulkily.)

Hoag: It's very nice of you to give me this time.

Gregg: No problem. Anything for Mr. Cigar.

Hoag: Lovely muskets. Do they work?

Gregg: Of course. No point in having them if they don't. I belong to a black powder shooting club. We frolic about the fields and streams exactly as they did a century ago. It's great fun. Sometimes we even wear underwear.

Hoag: I'd think ammunition would be hard to come by.

Gregg: I have it made.

Hoag: That you do. Own any contemporary arms?

Gregg: No, I don't bother to collect garbage. You like to spar, don't you?

Hoag: Not particularly.

Gregg: You're good at it.

Hoag: Everyone ought to be good at something. I've been hearing about the old days, when the band was starting up.

Gregg: The scruff days. And they were scruffs, Rory and Mr. Cigar. Their idea of a gas was to nick two air guns from a sports shop, go out to the junkyard, and let fly at the rats.

Hoag: Hit any?

Gregg: They did indeed. Right good shots they were. Brought their kills to school with them, so all of us could see.

Hoag: How tasteful of them. I understand you had a bit of a reputation yourself. Something about a pregnancy.

Gregg: Christ, he's not putting that in, is he? The girl, her parents adopted the baby. The boy still thinks his mum's his sister. "Boy." There's a laugh—he's thirty. I'm a grandpa, believe it? I've always sent the family a little money. Quietly. And I'd prefer it stay quiet, for the family's sake. You can understand, can't you?

Hoag: Yes, I can. However, that kind of decision isn't mine to make. If you want something left out I suggest you take it up with Tris. It's his book. Speaking of which, I have something rather delicate to ask, if you don't mind.

Gregg: I don't mind. I feel quite comfortable with you. It must be your eyes.

Hoag: What about them?

Gregg: They're sad. I don't trust happy people. They lie.

Hoag: Especially to themselves.

Gregg: You're very perceptive.

Hoag: I'm a helluva guy. Tris . . . he says you loved Rory. Is that true?

Gregg: (pause) Members of a band develop a closeness outsiders can't totally appreciate. We eat, sleep, bathe, and fuck in front of each other. We communicate with each other in our own language—the music. There's a bond. And there's love. I'm not ashamed to admit I loved Rory Law. He never fully returned it, but that never changed how I felt. Mr. Cigar threw it in my face when he learned of it. He could be cruel if he had something on someone.

Hoag: Did you and Rory ever. . . ?

Gregg: Have it off? Once, back in the crazy days. Chateau Marmont Hotel in Hollywood, '68 maybe, during one of those stoned-out after-concert orgy shows—the band and eight or ten groupies in a variety of configurations. Sexual experimentation was a vital part of the scene back then. Part of the adventure. Rory and me, we found ourselves together that night, and he looked at me and I looked at him and . . . he enjoyed it. He did. Though later he denied that, which hurt me. Is my gayness to be a part of this book?

Hoag: How would you feel about it?

Gregg: I'd absolutely love it. It'll be a gas, won't it?

Hoag: It'll open some eyes. How did it feel to be gay and yet be a sex symbol to millions of teenage girls?

Gregg: It was merely one part of a much larger illusion. We were never who the record company said we were. They made us up, like they did the old-time Hollywood movie stars. Christ, a lot of people still didn't know until he died of AIDS that Rock Hudson was gay. His studio had even married him off . . . Of course, early on, I was not a practicing homosexual. It simply wasn't done—at least, not among the working class. *(laughs)* I had my share of birds, and plenty of laughs. For a while. It just wasn't me, y'know? It was . . . it became very hard for me later on, traveling with Rory, wanting to make him happy, and seeing him destroy himself on drugs and stupid, greedy women. No woman ever made Rory happy, from when we were lads until the day he died.

Hoag: And Tris?

Gregg: Mr. Cigar never thought of women as people. Just things to fuck and forget.

Hoag: I very much want to understand him, but he's eluding me so far.

Gregg: He's the Shadow Man. You can't get inside of him. No one can. If you remember one thing you'll understand him as well as it's possible to: He was a bloke who was willing to do whatever it took to become a rock 'n' roll star. And that's a lot. And not all of it is pleasant. Rory, all he wanted out of life was to play his music and party. He cared nothing for the money or the business. He had his faults, of course. He was defiant, irresponsible, childish. But he was *right there.* Not Tris. He held back. He watched, calculated. Tris could chat up people who might do him good. He could sell himself. Rory couldn't. Tristam Scarr is an actor. He always has been an actor. I remember that first time he got up and sang at the Ealing Club for Alexis and Cyril—

Hoag: He was drunk. He told me about it.

Gregg: He was stone-cold sober. He *pretended* he was drunk so they would think he was some wild headstrong lad crazy with love for the music. He's shrewd. Always seems to know what the right move is, and never has trouble making it. He's not a nice man. It doesn't matter to him how he gets something. Just that he gets it. As we got more successful, he started asking this and that about the business end. Too late though. We had already been royally fucked over by Marco, who financed his other businesses with our profits and then told us we were broke. We had to pay Marco off with the rights to all of our early songs in order to get clear of our management agreement with him. He robbed us. They all robbed us . . . You've a job, Mr. Hoag. The only man who may have understood Mr. Cigar is dead. I doubt any woman knew him at all, except possibly for Tulip. I remember when they started going around together. She was the supermodel—beautiful, glamorous, socially connected. You couldn't pick up a mag without seeing her face on it. And she was still around after a few weeks, which was unheard of for Tris. When I asked him about her he said, "I don't feel like throwin' her out in the mornin'." That was all he had to say about the woman he married. Deep down, you see, the only person he's ever really loved is himself. I'll never forget the first time we played "I'm Walkin'," the Fats Domino song, at Crawdaddy. Mr. Cigar, he starts acting it out up there on stage—that was the night he invented The Strut, you see—and the girls, they start screaming over it, loving it. Excited him so much he got a raging hard-on right there on stage. He told me afterward he thought he was going to fire away right in his bleeding trousers . . . Rory, he lived for today. Tris, he lived for tomorrow. And now it is tomorrow, and there he is, all alone in the tower of his castle. Hasn't a mate in the world, y'know. Not one. Not that I'm being critical—I can afford to do anything I want, thanks to him. Did I mention I'm opening a conceptual art gallery next month at Beauchamp Place? I'll be featuring the work of Jeffrey, who you've just met. He's so very talented . . . I always admired Mr. Cigar, to be honest. I mean, it takes a terrific pair of balls to simply not care if everyone you know thinks you're an absolute shit. Like the business about dropping Jackie. When Marco approached us about taking Puppy into the group, Tris was the one who said yes. Didn't hesitate. He had to talk Rory into it. Had to talk Rory into pretending we were from the 'Pool, as well.

Hoag: How did you meet up with Marco?

Gregg: The Rough Boys basically broke up as a group after Mad Dog returned to America. Nothing formal. We just stopped playing together. Double Trouble went back to their vomitous little room and to hanging about the clubs. They jammed for a bit at Club 51with Jeff Beck, only Jeff and Tris didn't get along. Then Tris called me at the men's shop one day and asked me to meet him and Rory at Crawdaddy that night and to say nothing to Jackie about it. They were there with two men. One was about forty, and shaped more like a teapot than any person I've ever met. Marco Bartucci was also the first person I'd seen wearing muttonchop sideburns—still has them, I think. He was sweating profusely. Kept wiping his face and neck with a Western-style bandana.

Hoag: What was his background?

Gregg: He was raised in Glasgow of an Italian family. Said he'd worked for Larry Parnes in the fifties. Parnes was the promoter who brought along Tommy Steele and Johnny Gentle and Dickie Pride. I think Marco was some form of errand boy for him, though he claimed to have signed the Beatles for their very first road gig, opening for Johnny Gentle—before they were famous, of course. Lately, he'd been scouting talent in America, which is another way of saying he was waiting for something, or someone, to come along.

Hoag: And the man he was with?

Gregg: The other man was an American black in his early twenties. He had on a dark green suit of some shiny material, ruffled shirt and sunglasses, even though we were indoors and it was night. He wore grease in his hair to keep it straight. Chewed gum and kept tapping his fingers on the table. He was very wound up. Marco introduced him as Mad Dog Johnson's nephew, Albert, who went by the nickname Puppy and who played the drums. I said, "Pleased to meet you." He said, "Likewise." He spoke very softly, almost in a whisper. Marco had brought him over from America with the idea of making him into a rock 'n' roll star. See, there hadn't been a black rock star yet in Britain. Marco saw this as an opportunity.

Hoag: Smart.

Gregg: You'll never hear me call Marco stupid. What he had in mind was to put Puppy together with a young British R & B group. We came to mind because we'd toured with Mad Dog. I turned to Mr. Cigar and said, "What about Jackie?" And he replied, "Jackie's out." *(pause)* I was the one who told him. He wished us luck.

Hoag: Was Jackie upset?

Gregg: Why should he have been? He had no inkling of what was about to happen. Neither did I. Christ, I'll never forget the first time I heard Puppy play. A positively thrilling moment, it was. Puppy, he took the drums into an entirely new dimension. Made them into a lead instrument almost. Nobody played drums like Puppy did.

Hoag: Tris believes he was murdered.

Gregg: (laughs) That old business? He never gives up. It was foretold, or so he believes. He also happens to believe in flying saucers, gypsy curses, and voodoo.

Hoag: Foretold?

Gregg: The night before Puppy died some freaky witch who Rory used to drop acid with warned us that great tragedy was about to strike us. She saw it in her tarot cards or some such shit. Mr. Cigar, he took her warning seriously. Asked her if it was going to be some kind of accident—like getting bashed by a lorry—and she said no, it would be no accident. She said there was great hostility in the air. Christ, she was just some cow who painted her fingernails black. I can't believe he's still going on about that.

Hoag: You don't think Puppy was murdered.

Gregg: I know he wasn't. I was there. He took too much speed and drank too much champagne. That's what happened. Nothing more to it than that. Don't listen to Mr. Cigar.

Hoag: Jack agrees with him.

Gregg: Jack is loyal. And dim.

Hoag: He believes Puppy was done in by someone in the band, or close to it.

Gregg: That is just utterly absurd. Believe me, Mr. Hoag, Puppy's death was an accident. None of us killed him. It's absurd to even consider the idea. Puppy was our mate. Furthermore, he was our ace. He put money in our pockets. Why on earth would any of us have wanted him dead?

(end tape)

(Tape #1 with Marco Bartucci recorded in his office at Jumbo's Disco Nov. 26. Is casually dressed—wears an inferiority complex

in place of a necktie. Does look like a human teapot, with muttonchops. Is uneasy, hostile.)

Bartucci: What does T. S. want of me?

Hoag: Information. To fill out his recollections.

Bartucci: I see. So now he's asking me to help him sell books. Why should I? What have I to gain from it? Not that I'm a self-centered person.

Hoag: No, of course not. I think your interests will be served by talking to me. It's an opportunity for you to tell your side.

Bartucci: You want *my* side? Very well, here it is: whatever T. S. says about business I deny. Lies. All lies.

Hoag: Are you warm?

Bartucci: No, why?

Hoag: You're perspiring.

Bartucci: I always do. Means nothing.

Hoag: I understand you and the band came to a rather ugly parting over money.

Bartucci: I gave those boys everything, and for that, this terrible, unjustified smear continues to follow me about. As an example, the gentleman I've started this club with, my backers, they're Middle Eastern gentlemen, and they know very little about the past and Tris Scarr's groundless accusations. Now they're going to read about me and wonder.

Hoag: That shouldn't present a problem to you. The club seems to be doing quite well.

Bartucci: Thank you. I try.

Hoag: Unless . . .

Bartucci: Unless what?

Hoag: Unless you're stealing from them, too.

Bartucci: (silence) I'm afraid I don't like you, Mr. Hoag.

Hoag: It's a problem I run into fairly often.

Bartucci: T. S. hasn't changed. He's still the same rude, nasty boy who slurped his food and called anyone a cunt if they looked at him sideways. I can't stop him from saying what he wants. I never could tell him anything. He had total contempt for me. All rock musicians have contempt for their managers. They can't stand people who are responsible, but at the same time they expect someone to be responsible for them. And when things don't go exactly as promised, they scream bloody murder. A misunderstanding—that's all we had. I didn't steal from them—I *invested.* I made some mistakes. I'll admit to that. But if it hadn't been for me he'd still be hanging around Crawdaddy, playing for beer and smokes money. I made Us. He'll deny that, but it's a fact. They were a blues band going nowhere. Nobody wanted them. They needed direction. I gave it to them.

Hoag: Can you tell me about Puppy?

Bartucci: The boy never knew his real father, who was in jail for life. Mad Dog lived with the mother off and on, and helped to raise him. So he took Mad Dog's family name, and called him his uncle. He was a big, strong, muscular boy. He'd been a paratrooper in the army. Loved jumping out of airplanes. I remember once when he was very stoned in Stockholm he jumped out of a third-floor hotel window for fun. Broke both of his ankles. "The rush, man," he said, as we waited for the ambulance to arrive. "The rush." After the army, he got work on what they called the chitlin circuit, drumming for Little Richard, Ike Turner, the Isley Brothers. The first time I saw him he was playing at the Apollo Theater in Harlem behind some absolutely nothing soul singers. He was an unusually athletic drummer. Put on a show as well. He'd twirl a drumstick up in the air while he played, as if it were a baton. Or he'd spin 360 degrees around on his stool without missing a beat. Or he'd flick his tongue at the girls. I was taken by him. I went backstage and introduced myself. He was an up, good-humored boy. He mentioned that his Uncle Mad Dog was over here in Britain at the time being a famous American Negro blues artist. He was thinking about coming over here himself, just to see what it was like. I told him I was moving back soon, and that if he ever did come to look me up. And he did. He was finding it very strange being here. There were Jamaicans and Bahamians here at that time, but there were very few American blacks like Puppy. It was because of Puppy that Hendrix came over, you know. The two of them had played together in Harlem when they were very young. Puppy paved the way for Jimi, and for others. He was a revolutionary—not that he thought of himself that way. God no.

Hoag: What did you tell him when he showed up?

Bartucci: That I'd do what I could. Nothing came to me until I happened to bump into T. S. and Rory one evening soon after that at Crawdaddy. I knew them casually, to say hello.

Hoag: What were they like?

Bartucci: Talented. Cocky. Hungry. I happened to mention I knew someone they'd enjoy meeting, since they'd worked with Mad Dog. So the four of us got together for drinks, and the boys went crazy over him. He was, after all, their own age, yet he'd actually played with people like Little Richard, who was one of T. S.'s idols. They wanted to hear all about his experiences, all about Chicago and Memphis. Puppy was flattered. Also a bit overwhelmed. In America, white people knew very little then about blues performers like Son House and Leadbelly. The boys knew all of their songs. They talked to Puppy for hours. And then they heard him play.

Hoag: They were impressed.

Bartucci: Ginger Baker and Keith Moon were the very best of the young drummers around town then, Mr. Hoag. Puppy was so much better than them there was simply no comparison. T. S. and Rory watched him play, I swear, with their jaws down to here. They were dying to play with him, of course. I suggested that if they were serious that they think young and fresh as opposed to bluesy. And think about Liverpool. The 'Pool was *the* place then. The Mersey sound was *the* sound. So they got together with Derek and the four of them started playing together. And they cooked, right off. Toe-tapping music. Can't-sit-still music. It was Puppy. He made the difference. When they had it together I took them to Liverpool with a new name. We talked about promoting Puppy as Mad Dog's nephew, but the boys had already been down that blues road and failed at it, so we decided not to mention Mad Dog. When EMI signed them up, their people made out Puppy was the son of a Yank seaman who settled in the 'Pool after the war. They wanted the other boys to be from there as well, and to have scouse accents. Rory hated that part so much he elected to be the silent one.

Hoag: I always wondered why he let Tristam do all of the talking. I'm interested in your thoughts on Puppy's death.

Bartucci: What about it?

Hoag: Do you think he was murdered?

Bartucci: *(silence)* I never did believe his death was an accident.

Hoag: You didn't?

Bartucci: Because of Puppy's drug bust, Us was banned from appearing in America, where the major money was and still is. Without tour support, their record sales there slumped considerably. The ban wounded Puppy deeply. He offered to quit the group, let the others go on without him. They wouldn't hear of it, of course. They were fiercely loyal. Puppy was very, very down those last few weeks. That wasn't like him—ordinarily he was Mr. Up, Mr. Good Times. The parties, the drugs, the girls—they were always his doing. He was the instigator. That was why Tulip never cared for him. She thought he was a bad influence on T. S., who she was trying to turn into a gent. Puppy, he was a man of uncontrollable appetites, of major highs—and major lows. When a man like that gets down . . . It was no accident, his death. Puppy took his own life. Suicide. That's what I've always believed. Sad, really. Such a talent. So young.

(end tape)

CHAPTER SIX

That was the day my new suit was ready at Strickland's, so I stopped off after I finished with Marco and tried it on. It seemed to fit. So did Marco's explanation of Puppy's death.

Suicide. It made a lot of sense to me in this case. It certainly made more sense than Tris and Jack's murder plot. Like Derek had said: Why on earth would any of them have wanted Puppy dead? No reason, at least none that was apparent.

A ghost is brought in partly to keep a celebrity from making a consummate asshole out of himself. To that end, I decided I'd play down the murder theory in Tris's memoir—allude to it but not dwell on it. If I did, Tris would come off as paranoid and drugged-out. The critics would go after him. The book clubs would steer clear of him. Besides, there was plenty else for us to concentrate on, like Derek's gayness and his love for Rory. Definite bombshells. There would, I hoped, be more.

Illusion. No one was who they'd seemed to be. That was the Us story. What was Tris Scarr's story? I didn't know that yet. He was still peeling away like an onion—layer by layer, and with great difficulty. I was also getting the sinking feeling he was holding out on me, not letting me in on something about himself that was important. I had no idea what it was, or why I had this feeling.

He was the Shadow Man. What glimpses I'd gotten of him outside of his chamber had been few, and creepy. They were always at night, when he prowled the estate like a burnt-out lost soul. Once, I woke up to see him outside my window in the floodlit field behind the house, dressed in soccer shorts and cleats, intently kicking a soccer ball to an invisible goalie. Another night I saw—and heard—him careening through the maze like a human pinball on a Norton Commando 750cc motorcycle, bounding off hedges, splattering gravel. And once, while I was reading late at night by my sitting room fire, I heard the hall doorknob turn, then stop. When I went out in the hall, there was no one there. Only the smell of Gauloises.

He was the Shadow Man. How did the song go? "Don't come over to my side/You won't like what you see." What had he seen? I had to know. It was time to start beating on him. And to talk to Tulip. If only she would return my goddamned calls.

Lulu and I strolled along Savile Row, both of us blinking from the glare. It was the very first sunny afternoon since we'd arrived, and the city seemed completely different. Shiny. Bright. The air was fresh and tangy. The Christmas shoppers were smiling. It wasn't my London.

I got a haircut at Truefitt's in Bond Street from a tall, vaguely Indian-looking guy named Christopher. From there we headed over to the Saville Club on Brook Street. It's a stylishly run-down establishment that has a reciprocal arrangement with the Coffee House, where I sometimes go for lunch in New York. I had a lager and some ham sandwiches at the bar. Lulu had kippers. Then we started back to where we'd left the car. I was still watching for a tail—had been all day as I went from interview to interview. I was not being followed. I was quite sure of it.

It was when we were passing a corner newsstand that I spotted Merilee's picture—a publicity still from her show—and the screaming afternoon tabloid headline: "MERILEE SHE ROLLS ALONG!" I bought the paper and stood there and read it:

> Actress Merilee Nash, here to appear in the sold-out West End revival of *The Philadelphia Story* opposite Anthony Andrews, seems to find London just 'love-erly.'

The Oscar-winning American star has flown playwright-husband Zachary Byrd's coop and is snuggling with a tall, unidentified associate of our own Tristam Scarr.

Merilee and friend enjoyed a cozy opening night celebration at the Hungry Horse on Fulham Road, followed by a crawl through neighborhood pubs and a lengthy tête-á-tête outside her rented mews house on Crowell Road in an Austin Mini Cooper registered to the rock star.

Calls to T. S.'s home in Surrey, Gadpole, were in vain. "No comment," said a spokesman for the legendary rocker, who is reputed to be penning his memoirs for an American publisher. Several calls were placed to husband Byrd in New York. Byrd, Pulitzer Prize–winning author of the play *Labor Day*, was not available.

So that explained our tail that night. A member of the ever-vigilant British tabloid press had been shadowing Merilee. Part of me was relieved. Clearly, I wasn't in the middle of anything ugly or scary as it had first appeared. Part of me was wounded—the pride part. It's amazing how fast you can go from being a star to being a "tall, unidentified associate." Easiest thing in the world. All you have to do is nothing.

I tossed the paper in the trash.

I'd parked the mini on the corner where Clifford Street runs into Savile Row. I'd just started to unlock the car door when it happened. Actually, I didn't hear the first shot. What I heard, and saw, was the window exploding next to me. I wasn't quick to react. Just stared like an idiot at the shattered window, wondering how it could have happened. It wasn't until I heard the boom of a second shot and saw it blow out the back window beside my left elbow that I grabbed Lulu and hit the pavement. A tire popped a few inches from my head. The air hissed out. I could feel it on my ear. Someone was screaming now—a woman across the street. Then tires screeched and someone—whoever it was—sped away. Gone.

Slowly, I got to my feet. My hands were cut up from diving into broken glass, but otherwise I was okay.

Lulu wasn't.

If there's a sadder-faced creature in this world than a basset hound with a broken foreleg, I've yet to see it.

Merilee had made up a special bed for her in the mews house out of a crate and cushions, and placed it before the fireplace, which had a blaze going in it. There Lulu lay, bandaged, drugged, mournful. The gunshot had made a clean break. The vet had set it and kept her overnight at the pet hospital for observation. I had spent it tossing and shivering on the short love seat in Merilee's living room, wondering what I'd gotten myself into and eavesdropping as she assured Zack on her bedside phone that the tabloid story was a gross exaggeration and that she and I meant absolutely nothing to each other.

That wasn't what her green eyes had said when she bandaged up my hands in her tiny bathroom.

She was padding around in the kitchen now in old jeans, a Viyella shirt, and ragg socks, assembling Lulu's favorite meal—her mommy's tuna casserole. The kitchen was bright and high tech and the biggest room in the miniature house. The adjoining living room was barely big enough for the love seat and two companion armchairs, all of them of Fifties Moderne mustard-colored vinyl. I was busy in there entertaining Farley Root, a gawky, apologetic police investigator in his mid-thirties, with uncombed red hair, buckteeth, and an Adam's apple the size of a muskmelon. He wore a nile green three-piece polyester suit and had, possibly, the worst case of razor burn on his neck I'd ever seen. He looked like he shaved with a John Deere. He was perched on the love seat, sipping tea and trying hard to act cool even though the famous Merilee Nash was right there in the kitchen. He was also trying hard not to claw at his raw, itchy neck. He was failing at both.

Merilee came in with the teapot. "A warm-up, Inspector?"

He gulped some air. "Thank you, miss. Please. And I'm not actually an—"

"So what's this about, Inspector?" I asked. "More questions?"

A uniformed constable at the scene had already asked me the routine questions. He'd gotten the routine answers. I'd told him I had no idea why anyone had shot at me. The streets, we'd agreed, weren't safe anywhere anymore.

"Yessir," replied Root, pulling out a small notepad. "Sorry to bother you, Mr. Hoag. Just a few other matters I was interesting in pursuing. And, please, I'm not actually an—"

"No problem. And make it Hoagy."

"As in Carmichael?"

"As in the cheese steak."

He frowned. "Very well, Hoagy." He shifted on the love seat, gulped some more air. "It has come to our attention since you were questioned yesterday that you . . . you and Miss Nash, I mean . . . are perhaps in the midst of what could be called a domestic situation of a somewhat . . . uh . . ."

"Do you mean those awful tabloid stories?" Merilee asked, from the kitchen.

"I do, miss," he replied, relieved. "I don't mean to pry into your personal lives, but the press reports were followed by a shooting incident. One could draw the conclusion that—"

"My husband is in New York, if that's what you're wondering," she said. "Hoagy and I were once married, and we remain friends. That's all there is to the story. He's here now because of what happened to Lulu."

Lulu stirred in her bed at the sound of her name. Almost.

"Makes perfect sense, miss," said Root. "I-I do appreciate your candor, and being so understanding of my situation. I'm . . . allow me to assure you I've no interest in bothering you or invading your—"

"We understand," I assured him.

"Thank you, Hoagy," he said. "If I may take a bit more of your time . . . There was also this matter of the mini's owner. You say you're presently in the employ of . . ."

"Tristam Scarr. I'm helping him do his memoirs."

"You're a writer?"

I tugged at my ear. "Yes, I am."

"Any connection there, do you think?"

"My being a writer?"

He swallowed. "Do you think the shooting might have had to do with the work you're doing for Mr. Scarr?"

"I don't see how. It's just a collection of anecdotes about the old days, his views on his life. As I said yesterday, Inspector, I really can't think of anyone in London who would want me dead."

"I understand. And I'm not actually an—"

"But I will call you if I think of anything."

"Thank you, sir. Appreciate that. And I'll ring you if we turn up anything, though I can't say I'm optimistic."

"Not getting anywhere?"

"No one who witnessed the attack seems able to identify

precisely from where the shots originated, or to give us any description of who fired them. I'm afraid we don't even know so much as what kind of weapon was used." Root glanced at his notepad. "You mentioned you believe it was not a handgun."

"It sounded more like shotgun to me. It boomed."

"As does a large caliber handgun, such as a three-fifty-seven Magnum," Root pointed out.

"Could have been one of those," I conceded. "I would have thought you'd find a bullet, no?"

He shook his head. "The two that shattered the mini windows passed directly through the passenger-side windows as well. The one that clipped your hound here glanced off of the front tire and then passed underneath. As you had parked at an intersection, all three then proceeded on down Savile Row. They did not break any storefront glass. They do not appear to have glanced off any nearby buildings. We've found no glance marks. We're still searching, of course. However, it's a long street. And if the bullets happened to lodge in a pile of rubbish or in the side of a passing lorry, well, they may never be found."

"No spent cartridges anywhere?"

"No, sir. Whoever shot at you was neat and careful. Fired from their car, most likely. Gone before anyone really took notice of them."

"I don't imagine it was buckshot," I said. "Even if he'd had it on full choke there'd still be some pellet marks in the side of the car. From hitting Lulu, I mean."

Root nodded. "We're examining it. Nothing so far."

"I don't suppose anyone mentioned seeing a puff of smoke."

"Smoke? No. Why?"

"Just wondered."

Root tucked his notepad away in his coat pocket. "Yes, well, sorry to have troubled you."

"No trouble at all."

He struggled to his feet and lurched into the kitchen with his teacup. "Thank you so much for the tea, Miss Nash. It's been an honor to meet you. I've admired your work in films for many years."

"Why, thank you, Inspector," she said brightly.

He cleared his throat. "Actually, I'm not an—"

"You know, Inspector, I have an idea you might benefit from," I told him, as I steered him toward the front door. "Personally, I mean."

"Sir?"

"Talc." I fingered my neck. "Clear that rash right up. Floris makes one with a very light scent, number eighty-nine."

Root craned his neck uncomfortably. "Rather ugly business this. Can't seem to shake it. Number eighty-nine? Just may give it a go."

"Do you use an electric razor?"

"I do."

"They're murder."

"That they are. Good-bye, then."

"Good-bye, Inspector."

I knelt at Lulu's bed and scratched her ears. She treated me to her most profoundly pained look. A definite ten on the hankie meter.

"If you're trying to make me feel guilty," I told her, "you can stop now."

For that I got a whimper. A very weak whimper.

The casserole was bubbling away now in the kitchen. Merilee makes her tuna casserole with sautéed shallots and mushrooms, a touch of sherry, and a thick topping of melted Gruyère. She tasted it, frowned, and added a touch more sherry. I sipped the

Laphroaig I'd gone out for. It was strong and smoky. Possibly too smoky for me. I told Merilee I'd be taking Lulu back to Gadpole with me after she'd eaten.

"I can carry her," I said. "And she'll be fine on the train."

Merilee turned off the heat under the casserole and uncovered it. Lulu prefers it served tepid. "I think she should stay here, darling. At least for the weekend."

"What for?"

"She's comfy here. She's close to the hospital. And I don't think she's safe with you."

"Merilee, she'll be fine. There's no need to worry."

"That, Mr. Hoagy, is a load of baked beans. You were very nearly murdered. Both of you. Why didn't you tell that policeman what's really going on?"

"Because I don't *know* what's really going on." I poured myself another Laphroaig and Merilee some more of her cooking sherry. Of course, she cooks only with Tio Pepe. She won't put in food what she won't also drink. "Clearly, I am on to something—something that somebody wants to keep buried in the past. Maybe it's Puppy's death. Maybe it's something else. I don't know. I have to find out."

"And until you do you're putting her in danger."

"She'll be fine," I repeated.

Merilee sipped her sherry, unconvinced. "Why shoot at you? Why not T. S.?"

"I suppose because he's so well protected. It would also draw a lot of press attention. And speculation. This serves as a nice, quiet warning: Whoever did it is probably hoping T. S. will get scared and forget about the book."

"Will he?"

"I doubt it. My guess is that as long as T. S. personally feels secure he won't be bothered one bit."

Merilee put her hand against the casserole dish. It was no longer hot. She carried it over to Lulu's bed and presented her with the whole damned thing. None for his Hoagyness. "Here you are, sweetness," she cooed, patting her. "Now you eat this *awww* up so you can get s*twong* again."

Lulu pawed feebly at the dish with her good foreleg. Then she wriggled herself forward in her bed a bit and stuck her head in the dish. Chomping noises followed.

"This is truly low, Merilee. This is beneath you."

She frowned. "I really don't know what you mean, darling. I'm just giving her a little TLC."

"We agreed that I'd keep her. You got the apartment, the Jaguar—"

"And I'm not contesting it. But she's wounded, and my maternal instinct is taking over. I can't help it."

"You're trying to take her away from me."

"I'm not."

"She's my dog."

"She's our dog."

"She's *my* dog!"

A low moan emerged from Lulu's bed. She'd stopped eating and was watching us, genuinely distressed. It's true what they say—divorce is always hardest on the little ones.

"Merilee, I don't want to get into some kind of ugly, protracted custody battle with you."

"I don't want that either."

"Good. So I'll make this very simple: If she stays, I stay. We're a package deal. You take one, you get both."

Merilee raised an eyebrow, the same one she raised when Mel Gibson made his play for her in that sweaty tropics melodrama they did together. Her only flop. On screen, that is. "Now who's getting low?"

I went to her and took her in my arms. She didn't resist. "I got a stiff neck sleeping on the love seat last night."

"It *is* short."

"Your bed isn't."

She sighed. "Hoagy . . ."

"Yes, Merilee?"

She pulled away, went to the closet, and came back with her red Converse Chuck Taylor high-tops and her mink. "Let's walk."

Kensington Gardens was where we went. It was a Saturday afternoon and there were people there—pipe-puffing dog walkers, loners with their shoulders hunched and their hands in their pockets, young couples with baby strollers. It wasn't like being in Central Park. No trash. No graffiti. No dead rats lying in the walkway. No teenage roller skaters with boom-boxes. Also, no one carrying shotguns. This I could be fairly sure of. I was looking. Getting shot at will do that to you.

We walked in silence alongside the Serpentine, enjoying the quiet, until we came upon a young father teaching his little boy how to ride a bicycle. The boy was chubby and apple-cheeked, and wore a tweed cap.

"Oh, darling," exclaimed Merilee, squeezing my arm. "I want one of those."

I coughed. "A midget human life-form?"

"No, one of those caps."

"Oh. Somewhat oversized, I assume."

"Yes. Would you. . . ?"

"Would I what, Merilee?"

"Would you buy it for yourself and then give it to me?"

I took her to Bates, a tiny, cluttered old hat shop on Jermyn Street. The proprietor's cat from much earlier in the century still stood guard there from inside a glass case—properly stuffed, of course. It wouldn't be long before the clerk who fitted me would be joining Puss in there himself, I reckoned. I got a charcoal gray herring-bone tweed that would have gone nicely with my new suit, and presented it to Merilee when we got outside on the sidewalk. She tried it on right away, admired her reflection in the store window from one angle, then another. Then she burst into tears.

I held her until they stopped. Then I gave her my linen handkerchief and asked, "What is all this?"

She dabbed at her face with the handkerchief. "All this," she replied, sniffling, "is that I'm still in love with you. I didn't sleep a wink all night. I couldn't. All I could do was think about how much I want you back."

I'd been waiting three years to hear Merilee say those words. Now that she had I found myself feeling just a little dubious. "I see," I said quietly.

She eyed me. "Well, don't jump up and down," she said drily.

"I won't."

"What's wrong? Are you thinking it's just because of Lulu?"

"You're the one who said your M-instinct has been aroused."

"It's not all that's been aroused."

"Actually, I was thinking about Tracy."

"What's Tracy got to do with it?"

"Merilee, you do happen to be playing a woman who does happen to fall back in love with her ex-husband."

She mulled this over, as we stood there on Jermyn Street. "There is that," she conceded. "I *am* an actress, and therefore a nut. This whole situation is rather . . ."

"Neat?"

"And it's bothering you."

I shrugged. "My professional nutsiness drove us apart. I suppose it's entirely appropriate if yours brings us back together. I guess I can handle it. Just promise me one thing."

"Name it."

"Don't ever do *Macbeth.* Not even if Papp begs."

She laughed girlishly. "Papp doesn't beg."

We kissed. It started soft and sweet, but didn't stay that way for very long.

She pulled away, gasping. "Darling, we're being indiscreet."

"So?" I gasped back.

"Not fair to Zack."

I caught my breath, looked around. People on the street were indeed watching us. "You're absolutely right. Let's go somewhere nice and quiet, and get discreetly naked."

We didn't stray far from the feathers the rest of the weekend. Lulu seemed cheered by our reconciliation. She even started to hop around the house a bit, which meant now I *had* seen something sadder than a basset hound with a broken foreleg—a basset hound with a broken foreleg trying to walk. Not that she's particularly gutsy. This was strictly a ploy for sympathy. And smoked salmon.

Merilee and I had one ground rule. We would talk only about London. No talking about afterward allowed. But there was no ordinance against thinking about it, and that's what I did as we cuddled there in the middle of the night, all cozy and warm under our down comforter and tray of salmon sandwiches and cocoa. I let myself think about Zack out and me back in. Back in the eight art deco rooms overlooking the park. Back in the sweet life—acclaimed, promising, madly in love. Maybe you can't go back, but you can always try. Hmm. Maybe here was the ending for novel number two. A *happy* ending.

I let myself think about us. Sure I did.

Monday morning the dampness and gray skies were back. Merilee showed me to the door wearing my old silk target dot dressing gown. It definitely looked better on her than it did on me, especially with nothing on underneath it. I undid the sash, opened it wide and probed its contents, purely for the sake of scientific analysis. She pressed against me and let me feel her warmth and her strength. Then she stood on her toes and put her mouth to my ear.

"Come back, darling," she whispered.

"I don't think you need to worry about that."

I scratched Lulu's neck and told her to stay off the paw. She didn't argue with me. She was going to stay there with Merilee for the time being. It did make sense not to move her. Besides, I'd be back as often as I could manage. I'd have to bring Lulu's vest. Also my new target dot dressing gown, so Merilee and I could lounge about the mews house in our his-and-his robes.

It was Jack's day off. Pamela met me at the Guildford station in the Silver Cloud. She was outfitted in a mannish black pants suit, white shirt, and black necktie, all of this topped off by a black chauffeur's cap. I rode up front with her, and immediately regretted it. She drove like a demon.

"You'll be pleased to learn," she announced, rounding a corner with a screech of rubber, "that I've finished typing up the transcripts of your tapes with Mr. Scarr."

"Excellent." Among her myriad other talents, Pamela typed a hundred and twenty words per minute, and none of them were Etaoin Shrdlu. "Pamela, I think we should talk seriously about your coming back to New York with me when I'm done here."

"My Lord, Hoagy," she exclaimed, blushing. "It's been years since I've received such an indecent proposition from such a young gentleman."

"Not so young. And not so indecent. My ex-wife and I—what I mean is, we may be looking for someone."

"So you two *are* together again."

"Why, yes. How did you—?"

"It was I who spoke with the gossip sheet when they rang

up. They'd traced the number off of the mini. I told them nothing, of course."

"I appreciate your discretion."

"I've plenty of practice, believe me. I spoke to the police as well."

"So did I."

Pamela sped through the traffic with the lunatic zeal of a Canarsie-born cabbie. At one intersection a truck driver had to hit his brakes hard to keep from plowing into us. He shook his fist at her.

She clucked at him and said, "I've never been to New York."

"You'll do just fine."

"I was so sorry to learn of Miss Lulu's misfortune. Is she better?"

"Actually, she's getting seriously spoiled."

"Do give her my best."

She made the trip to Gadpole in half the time it took Jack. We had passed through the main gate and were cruising through the cluster of staff houses and service buildings when I heard the sharp crack of pistol fire. Then silence. Then more pistol fire. I shuddered, remembering just how close those shots had come the other day.

"Jack executing some of the help?" I asked.

"Getting in some target practice, I expect."

"I'll get out here, if I may."

"You may."

Behind some gardeners sheds, two targets were set into a twenty-foot-high mound of earth. Jack stood fifty feet away, firing off bull's-eyes with a twenty-two-caliber target pistol. So did another shooter, who was tall and lean and dressed in matching camouflage safari jacket, fatigue trousers, and baseball cap. It wasn't until I got up closer behind them that I realized the other crack shot was that precocious little multimaniac herself, Lady Vi.

They didn't notice me there until they stopped to reload, and I said, "You're rather good, Violet."

She treated me to a devilish grin and pointed her gun at me. "Bang bang."

Jack snatched it from her. "Never, ever point a weapon at someone, Vi! I've told you!"

"It's empty!" she protested.

"No matter whether it is or it isn't," he lectured sternly. "You could be mistaken. And *most* sorry."

Just to satisfy himself, Jack pointed the empty gun at one of the targets and pulled the trigger.

It wasn't empty.

He stood there staring at the hole he'd made in the target. Then he looked down at the gun in his hand and, slowly, up at me, horrified.

"Yet another bull's-eye," I observed with a brave smile and jelly knees. Clearly, I'd have to steer wide of guns for a while. Also cracks in sidewalks, black cats, and precocious, long-limbed teenagers.

This one was tickled thoroughly pink. "Just having a bitty goof," she exclaimed with a merry laugh as she grabbed her empty gun back from a still-stunned Jack. "Can't a girl have a goof?"

"I don't see why not," I replied graciously. Jack and I watched her reload the target pistol. "And how is she with a sporting rifle?" I asked him.

"Even better," he replied softly.

"But not as good as Jackie," she pointed out. "No one's as good as Jackie."

"Taught her m'self," he said. "Since she was a little thing." He stuck a hand out to me. "Allow me to welcome you back, sir." Happy to see you're all of a piece. How's the pup?"

"Not very happy," I replied, shaking his hand.

"Poor little bugger," he said.

"Sorry about the mini," I said. "Quite a car."

"Indeed, sir. I'll have her towed back here soon as they're done with her. Get her put back together good as new. You're welcome to the Peugeot, in the meantime." Jack swiped at his nose with the back of his hand. "Terrible business, this. I know Mr. Scarr is most upset."

"Yes, I should think he would be," I said quietly.

Jack's eyes narrowed. We stood there staring at each other.

Violet broke in, offering me her gun, barrel down. "Care to shoot a round?"

"Thank you, no," I replied. "Javelin is more my style."

"Javelin?" she asked, frowning. Evidently she wasn't too up on track and field, which was probably just as well. Who knew what havoc she could wreak with a discus.

"It's a spear," I explained. "Long. With a point at the tip."

"Ooh, sounds fun."

"Somehow," I said, "I had a feeling you'd think so."

It was time to get out my mukluks. I always wear them when I'm at the typewriter. I wore them when I was writing the novel, and I don't dare change now. There's no telling where inspiration comes from. Who's to say it isn't footwear?

I put on *It's Us Again* good and loud to get myself in the mood. The album was recorded after the group's first American tour. "More for Me" was its big hit. I set out the tape transcripts and notes, sat at the desk and put a sheet of paper in the typewriter. Almost at once I was aware that something was missing—Lulu always sleeps under the desk when I work, with her head on my foot. I got up, pulled a heavy tome from the bookcase, and tried resting that on my foot. It wasn't warm and I couldn't feel it swallow, but the weight was right. Much better. Don't ever tell Lulu that she was replaced by Anthony Trollope.

I like to set the tone of a memoir with an introductory chapter that takes place in the present. This lets the reader know right off what the celebrity's attitude is toward the life and career he or she is about to look back on. It gives everybody a handle, including me. Unfortunately, I couldn't do this with T. S. I didn't have the handle yet. In a perfect world, I would have waited until I did before I started writing. It's not a perfect world. Publishers have deadlines.

So I started with Tris's account of his childhood. I covered his early memories of his parents and Rory and getting hooked on Brando, Elvis, and the music. I took it up through the formation of the Rough Boys and those nights spent jamming in the lorry garage. I gave him a tough, uncompromising voice peppered with coarse language and the hint of a sneer. It was the voice that came through on the tapes. It was his voice.

I just wished I knew what he wasn't telling me about himself. I was starting to take it personally.

Dinner was a roast chicken, in the kitchen with Pamela. I asked her a bunch of questions about how many invisible people it took to maintain Gadpole (thirty-three) and what all of them did. Eventually, I cleverly managed to bring the conversation around to Jack.

On Friday afternoon, when someone had decided to use me, the mini, and Lulu for target practice, Jack Horner had been out, she said. Running errands in Guildford.

And Miss Violet? The irrepressible Lady Vi had been posing for a British *Vogue* layout the entire day. In London.

I turned in early, but I didn't get to sleep. For one thing, there was too much to think about. Had it been Jack who'd shot at me? He *had* been flatly opposed to my poking around in the past.

Violet? Clearly, she was less than stable. Maybe she hadn't coped too well with my rejecting her. True, I'd heard a car speed away from the shooting scene, and she wasn't yet old enough to drive. But she wasn't old enough to do a lot of the things she no doubt did. Operating a vehicle without a license was probably the least of her sins. And then there were the others. Derek. Marco. Even T. S. himself, not that he got out much. Who was it? What was I in the middle of? How was I going to find out?

The other reason I couldn't get to sleep was Lulu. I was used to her sleeping on my head. I tried putting a pillow over my face but it just wasn't the same. Didn't smell like mackerel.

So I watched the videocassette of *This is the Beginning of the End* that I'd borrowed from T. S. This was the infamous Stanley Kubrick black-and-white documentary chronicling the Us '76 American tour. Their last tour. They were older now, Double Trouble were. They'd had the breakups and the crack-ups, and it showed. T. S. and Rory were no longer two wild kids. This was business now, and they were two polished pros giving their audience what it wanted. Kubrick captured that—just how much backstage preparation and role-playing and outright deception went into creating the onstage illusion of spontaneous good times. And Kubrick got more than that, more than he or anyone bargained for. His cameras were there that hot, humid night in Atlanta. There as T. S. and Rory were on the Omni stage in their torn sleeveless T-shirts, and spandex pants, faces and chests gleaming with sweat. T. S., clutching a hand mike, is strutting around the stage, taunting the screaming audience as he snarls out their encore, "We're Double Trouble." Rory, grinning his snaggle-toothed grin, is straining for a note on his Stratocaster. He finds it. Leaps in the air with joy. The crowd is on its feet now, pressing towards them. And then suddenly there is a flash of light and Rory's face contorts even more. Straining for another note, isn't he? All part of the show, isn't it?

No, it's not. Blood is streaming from Rory's mouth and nose now. He is crumpling. Falling onto the stage floor. The camera is jostled, and for a moment we're looking at someone's booted feet. There are screams. Screams that change abruptly from adulation to horror. Derek shoves forward, points into the crowd, and yells. He can't be heard over the mounting shrieks.

The camera finds the shooter there in the third row, brandishing his gun, eyes crazed, spittle bubbling from his lips. There he is—Larry Lloyd Little, witness for the prosecution in the Manson trial. Fringe family member. Pimp. Out of jail after three years. Flashbulbs explode. He's babbling something. Original sin, he is saying. Or so the press later reported. Original sin. And he won't drop the gun. And the police are firing on him now, and he's hit. He goes down, terrified fans scrambling to get out of his way as he falls. And we hear a voice now in the erupting chaos, a voice from the stage crying "Help him! Can't somebody please help him!" It's a voice we've never heard before. It's the real voice of T. S. He's dropped his fake scouse accent. The act is forgotten as he kneels over his dying partner. Rory lies there on his back. His eyes are open. Derek is there. So is Jack, and Corky Carroll, the tour drummer. Then the ambulance arrives and the paramedics put him on a stretcher and take him away. T. S. is now alone there on stage. Rory's blood is on his hands. He's looking around, bewildered, lost. Derek comes over, tries to comfort him. "Why?" T. S. keeps saying. "Why?"

I hadn't seen the movie in a long time. It seemed even more powerful to me now, for a lot of reasons.

I was still awake at three a.m. when I heard a door open and close down the hall. Violet's door. I slipped my trench coat on over my nightshirt, quietly opened my own door, and stuck my head out into the dimly lit hallway. No one. Just the sound of footsteps—reaching the stairs, going down the stairs. I followed, stepping lightly. It was so silent in the great house I could hear the mice scratching around in the walls. I started down the curved staircase. The footsteps were on the marble floor now, heading toward the kitchen. A late-night snack?

There was no one in the kitchen. Just the hum of the refrigerators. The pantry door, however, was open an inch. Pamela always kept it closed. No one was in there, but the door to the herb garden was unbolted. I stepped outside into the cold. No palace guard seemed to be stationed here, and it was dark—a blind spot in the security floodlights. I heard the gate to the vegetable garden squeak, and the soft crunch of gravel under feet. I pursued through the gardens until I came to a stone fence about four feet high. This I climbed over.

I was in a small meadow behind the garages. Ahead of me, in the darkness I could just make out Violet striding briskly toward them. She went inside a back door to the utility garage, which connected to Jack's apartment.

His lights were on. I found a window that had a nice view of his parlor. Jack was sitting in a lounge chair in front of the fireplace, which had an electric space heater inserted in it. Violet stood before him with her head bowed like a penitent child. He was gesturing sharply at her, and she was apologizing. I couldn't hear the words through the window. Until he raised his voice:

"You know what happens to bad girls, don't you?"

"I *said* I was sorry, Jackie! *I did!*"

He grabbed her roughly by the arms, pulled her across his lap and yanked her sweatpants down, exposing her round, firm, altogether perfect young bottom. This he spanked with his meaty hand. Hard. She yelped. She yelped each time he smacked her, which was either six or seven times. She began to sob. Then Jack said something to her. Whatever it was, it made her giggle. Then she sat up and put her arms around his neck and kissed him, and he carried her into the bedroom.

CHAPTER SEVEN

(Tape #5 with Tristam Scarr. Recorded in his chamber Nov. 29. Wears bathrobe and slippers. Is very agitated.)

Scarr: They still have no idea who shot at you?

Hoag: None. Do you?

Scarr: Me? Why should I have any idea?

Hoag: Well, there's your little theory about Puppy's death to consider.

Scarr: (pause) So he *was* murdered. I'm right. Have been all along. And whoever it is is afraid I'll say something, aren't they?

Hoag: I want you to know I don't scare easily, Tristam. I scare *very* easily.

Scarr: You'll be quitting then.

Hoag: That's up to you.

Scarr: Me?

Hoag: Oh, for Christ's sake—let's stop jerking each other's chains, shall we?

Scarr: Giving me something of an attitude, aren't you, mate?

Hoag: I don't think so. I've gotten shot at. *Me*, not you. I have a right to know why, and you're not telling me.

Scarr: I've told you everything I—

Hoag: Who killed Puppy?

Scarr: I already told you! I don't know!

Hoag: Bullshit.

Scarr: Don't push me, mate! When T. S. says he doesn't know, he means it.

Hoag: More bullshit.

Scarr: What is it you want? A punch-up?

Hoag: What I want is the truth.

Scarr: I repeat: I do not know who killed Puppy.

Hoag: Okay. Fine. Duly noted. I don't know if I believe you or not, but I suppose that's my own problem.

Scarr: Why won't you believe me?

Hoag: I'll tell you why—because I don't know you. We may have spent some hours together talking, but I still don't know you. And until I do there's no such thing as trust.

Scarr: *(silence)* You're trying to relate me to your terms. They don't apply. I'm not anyone else. I'm T. S.

Hoag: And who is T. S.?

Scarr: He's . . . I'm . . . someone who's monstrously, royally, fucked up. And always have been. Okay?

Hoag: How?

Scarr: Christ! *(long silence followed by sounds of heavy breathing)* Ever since I was a lad, alone in m'room, I've felt . . . *(sounds of heavy breathing sniffling) apart.* Isolated. I-I was often sick, as I told you . . . But . . . But . . .

Hoag: Yes? Go on.

Scarr: What I didn't tell you was . . . There was this thing inside m'head. This terror. It would last for days, weeks. Total fucking freak-out. I couldn't eat or sleep. I'd get headaches. So bad I couldn't keep m'eyes open. I'd just sit there in the dark, alone. I-I still get them. Had one last week. A bad one.

Hoag: You did seem a little out of it.

Scarr: I thought money and fame would make it all go away. That's what drove me to make it in music. I was wrong. None of it has ever gone away. That's the biggest disappointment of my life . . . All the drugs, they just made it worse. Acid very nearly destroyed me. Made me so bleedin' paranoid I-I couldn't believe in anyone, especially if they wanted something of me—and everyone wanted something of me . . . I've never been one to take things as they come, see the good in them. I'm totally preoccupied by the bad. The truth is I never enjoyed any of my success. I'm not capable of it. And that has made me want to lash out at people, destroy what I was building.

Hoag: Did you ever get professional help?

Scarr: My unconscious is the heart and soul of my creativity. I could never let someone fuck with it. I've always been looking for answers on my own. It's taken me a long fucking time to realize there just aren't any.

Hoag: Did Rory know this about you?

Scarr: He didn't understand it, but he knew of it, from when we were lads. M'glums, he called it. Rory, he was the only one who could sometimes pull me out of it. He was my mate. My only true mate. When I lost him, I just freaked out. Most people thought I retired because I was afraid of being shot myself. That was only a part of it. It was losing Rory. I still feel his . . . his *loss (sounds of weeping, then silence)* Christ . . . Haven't had a good bleedin' cry in don't know how long. Sorry about all of this, Hogarth.

Hoag: Congratulations, Tristam.

Scarr: For?

Hoag: For breaking through—from the public you to the private you. This has been far and away our most important night's work. I'd say it calls for a drink, my friend.

Scarr: This goes in the book?

Hoag: It does.
Scarr: I don't know if I—
Hoag: Trust me.
Scarr: (pause) Sancerre do?
Hoag: Always has.
Scarr: You haven't a glass, Hogarth.
Hoag: Another cause for celebration—you finally noticed.

(end tape)

(Tape #6 with Tristam Scarr. Recorded in his chamber Nov. 30. Still wears robe and slippers.)

Scarr: I've read the pages you sent up. I like it so far. Very much.

Hoag: I'm glad.

Scarr: You don't think there's too much soul-searching about the laddie days?

Hoag: It's dynamite.

Scarr: If you say so.

Hoag: Good man. I'd like to hear about Liverpool.

Scarr: It was gray and depressed and nowhere—unless you happened to be a rocker. The Mersey sound had taken over the charts. Brian Epstein's doing, actually. Aside from the Beatles, he'd brought along Gerry and the Pacemakers, who had two number ones, "How Do You Do It?" and "I Like It." Then Billy J. Kramer did "Do You Want to Know a Secret?," a Lennon-McCartney song, and that went to the top as well. There was The Searchers, Cilia Black . . . The 'Pool's where it was at. London wasn't, at least not for us.

Hoag: How long did you live up there?

Scarr: A week.

Hoag: Wait, I thought you—

Scarr: Moved up there? No. We got it together around home. Found ourselves a new name. Most people thought Us had to do with racial harmony or like that. Actually, it came from sitting around one night with a list of twenty-five names and liking that one the best. Marco staked us to some better equipment. Fender Strato for Rory, Fender Precision Bass for Derek. Vox AC thirty amps. We started out by playing a lot of the songs we'd been playing, only more up-tempo. That was Puppy's influence. He was totally up. Had what I call The Energy, y'know? And he was so bleedin' good we figured we'd give him a couple of drum solos. No band had done that before. When we had it together we took the train up and checked into a cheap hotel. Marco knew Ray McFall, who owned the Cavern, which the Beatles had made famous. Got us a gig there. A dingy jazz cellar in the city center, it was, walls dripping with sweat. Record company executives in suits were queued up to get in the door, hoping lightning would strike the same place twice. What did they know about the music? They knew shit . . . We'd been at it for years, y'know? When it finally did happen for us, it happened *bam*—EMI offered us a contract on the spot. They'd signed the Beatles. When they got wind we weren't actually locals they figured as how we should say we were, as did Marco. He handled the contracts. Gave each of us an allowance. We were bleedin' louts about the business end. Signed whatever the fat little cunt put in front of us. Fucked us royally, he did . . . We cut our first single at the EMI Studios in London. George Martin, the Beatles' producer, was our producer as well. Very polite. Also very much the big boss man. Told us "Great Gosh Almighty" would be our first single, with "Shake, Rattle and Roll" as the B-side. Told us Puppy's drum solos didn't fit. Told me to leave m'harp in m'pocket. The entire thing was over in four hours. Then the hype started. Marco gave us Beatles haircuts and gold blazers and new identities. Derek was the Face, Rory the Serious Musician, Puppy the Joker. I was the Talker. I was always to put on the scouse accent. Got to be second nature, after a while. What took getting used to was the things they started planting about us in *Rave* and *Fabulous*, the teeny fan mags, like who our favorite film stars were and what we ate for breakfast. I mean, they never even asked us. Then they put us in a cinema hall package tour, opening for the Everly Brothers in Northampton, Leicester, Nottingham . . . That's when it started to pop for us. It was the girls, mostly. It was how they responded to Puppy.

Hoag: How did they respond?

Scarr: They screamed. Tried to climb up on the stage. Rushed the stage door afterward, wanting to meet him, touch him. I mean, the man was doing some very sexy, outrageous things up there. Inflaming 'em. He was *black,* mate. The boyfriends, they tore up their seats. Threw rocks and bottles at the coach as we pulled away. Rioted, practically. Marco, he milked it, started alerting the police and newspapers in each town before we arrived. That got us the "Fear Jungle-Boy Riot" headlines. Turned us into a sensation. The police had to form a human chain in front of the stage every night. And "Great Gosh Almighty" went to number three on the charts.

Hoag: How did Puppy react to all of this?

Scarr: He was a performer. He loved the attention, particularly from white girls.

Hoag: How did you and Rory feel about this—that this is what it took to put you over the top?

Scarr: This was our shot, mate. We didn't care how we got it. The important thing was what we did with it once we had it. Plenty of groups came and went with their one hit, their one gimmick. Staying hot, that was something else. Had to keep the hits coming, one after another. Only a handful of groups managed that—the Beatles, Stones, the Who, and Us.

Hoag: What did it take?

Scarr: No great mystery there. To stay on top, a group had to grow musically. Had to care about the music, not just the trappings. Fight for the music, which meant you telling the record company what to do, rather than them telling you. Rory and me, we wrote our first song together in the motor coach between Sheffield and Leeds. I put some lyrics down. He strummed some chords. We hummed a melody, and soon we had something—"Come on Over, Baby." We recorded it soon as the tour ended. Now that Puppy was a celebrity, George Martin let us include a drum solo. And I played m'harp. "Come on Over, Baby" shot to number one. That got us a spot on *Ready, Steady, Go*, the top telly program. And it got us released in North America.

Hoag: You mentioned the Beatles, Stones, The Who. You go back a lot of years together. Your readers will be interested in your thoughts on them.

Scarr: The music?

Hoag: The people.

Scarr: I don't know about that, Hogarth . . .

Hoag: Let's try a word association. I give you a name, you tell me what pops into your mind. *(pause)* Lennon . . . *(silence)* Jagger . . . *(silence)*

Scarr: Look, I'd rather not do this. I don't wish to write about my mates in this book. I really don't.

Hoag: Derek said you have no mates.

Scarr: Did he? I could get a hundred of them here in thirty minutes. All I have to do is ring them up.

Hoag: So why don't you?

Scarr: *(silence)* Perhaps I will one day soon. Perhaps I will.

Hoag: I'll be looking forward to it.

(end tape)

(Tape #2 with Derek Gregg. Recorded at his new art gallery, The Big Bang Theory, Nov. 30. Workmen are still in process of unfinishing it—walls and ceiling are being stripped to bare brick and exposed pipes. And left that way.)

Hoag: Interesting decor.

Gregg: Perfectly dreadful, isn't it? Whatever's in, I always say.

Hoag: I'd like to talk about what was "in" here in '64, when you first hit it big.

Gregg: They called it Swingin' London, luv. We were a part of it. But it was bigger than us. It was a wave of new talent that was shaking up just *everything.* Actors like Michael Caine and Terence Stamp. Fashion designers like Mary Quant, with the miniskirt. David Bailey, the photographer, was changing the meaning of glamour, and models like Tulip were changing the meaning of beautiful. She asked about you, by the way. I said you were okay. She'll see you.

Hoag: That's terrific. Thanks. Are you two close?

Gregg: We all remain close—we went through a revolution together. Suddenly, it was hip to be a commoner, to be loutish, untutored, real. Suddenly, we were the celebrities. The photographers followed us day and night. The more the older generation put us down, the more the young ones wanted to be just like us. We rolled around in it, we did. Shit, we were twenty-two. We dressed flash and behaved flash. Drank and partied all night at the Ad Lib Club and Bag O' Nails. Each of us had three or four different flats where we crashed with three or four different girls. Even me. Treated them all the same—"Hang out, doll. Maybe I'll be back." Mr. Cigar, he emerged as this major spokesman on public issues. "Who'd you be voting for in the upcoming election?" they'd ask him. "Donald Duck," he'd reply, and it would be on the front page the next day. I remember he said to me one night that if he stuck two lit Woodbines up his nostrils, every teeny in Great Britain would start smoking his cigarettes like that . . . We had *power.* That's what it was. It was a trip. I miss it.

Hoag: After "Come On Over, Baby" was released in the U.S., you—

Gregg: We went on over, yes, and it was a big disappointment. Here at home we had a number one song. There, we were merely another new British group. There were no screaming girls when we landed. No press conference. Nothing. Mr. Cigar wanted to fire Marco on the spot, he was so pissed off. We stayed at an overheated salesman's hotel on Thirty-Fourth Street, the New Yorker. We did not get booked on *The Ed Sullivan Show* or play Carnegie Hall. We were on the radio with some guy called Murray the K, and our gig was at a discotheque in Times Square called The Cheetah. But we did go over well there. Met recording people. Also met the Warhol crowd, and fell in with them. Went down to that utterly bizarre place of his, The Factory, where we got turned on to marijuana. Mr. Cigar started his thing with Edie Sedgewick then. I personally had my first gay experience with someone I met there. Through Puppy we met Jimi Hendrix, who was playing at a basement dive in Greenwich Village. He blew us away with his music. He and Rory were both guitar freaks—spent hours together in the guitar shops on West Forty-Eighth Street. New York was a happening place. But once we left there, Christ, it was like being back in the northern provinces. In Philadelphia we lip-synched "Come On Over, Baby" on the *American Bandstand* program, and also appeared on a chat show called *The Mike Douglas Show.* The host had been a big band singer, so he thought it would be a gas to put on a Beatles wig and join us. Rory simply handed the fellow his Strato and walked off. God, he hated that shit . . . From there we hit the road in a rented motor coach, with Jack at the wheel. Marco had booked us on a tour of the South, playing auditoriums and fairgrounds in places like Birmingham and Jackson where the civil rights thing was really quite volatile. The idea was that Puppy's antics would set off the same fireworks they had back home in the north.

Hoag: Did they?

Gregg: Too much so. After our first couple of appearances our gigs were canceled in a lot of cities down the road. Too risky, they called us. That got us some national attention, made Pup a cause célèbre. When we arrived in Los Angeles we even got invited—dig this—to a dinner party at Sammy Davis Jr.'s home. It was a show of racial support for Pup by the liberal show-biz crowd, or some such thing. Blew us away—all of these famous Hollywood stars like Sidney Poitier, Gregory Peck, and Natalie Wood showed up there to support us. Mr. Cigar freaked out over meeting Natalie Wood, with her having been in *Rebel Without a Cause.* He asked her all about James Dean. Then he took her home and fucked her. And told *everyone* . . . Tris was really taken by America. He particularly took to the glamour and unsavoriness of L.A.—Grauman's Chinese Theater, Disneyland, Marilyn Monroe's grave. He ended up living in Malibu for a few years when we got into tax trouble. I chose the Italian Riviera. To each his own . . . Do they know yet who shot at you?

Hoag: Planning to confess?

Gregg: (laughs) You have a wonderful sense of humor. That bothers me about Jeffrey. He's so solemn. So *dumb.*

Hoag: On the face of it, it couldn't have been you. You're strictly a black powder man.

Gregg: And?

Hoag: Three shots were fired at me in the space of no more than ten seconds. Can't do that with a muzzle loader—it takes too long to reload. You've got your powder, your wadding, your ball. Then you've got to push all of that down with your ramrod. No way it was done with a muzzle loader. At least, not a *standard* muzzle loader.

Gregg: Meaning?

Hoag: If I remember correctly, they made a few single-barrel muzzle loading *repeaters* with superimposed loading. Mostly experimental. Very hard to find now. Museums have them, a few wealthy collectors. Do you own one?

Gregg: (silence) No, I own two—an 1828 Jenning/Reuben T. Ellis Repeating Flintlock four-shot and an 1863 Lindsay Repeating Percussion Rifle-Musket.

Hoag: Make quite a puff of smoke, don't they?

Gregg: They do. What of it?

Hoag: Then again, you *could* have done the job simply by using three different standard muzzle loaders, all of them loaded and at hand . . . Couldn't you?

Gregg: You don't actually believe *I'm* the one who shot at you, do you?

Hoag: You did seem pretty upset about Tris mentioning your child in the book.

Gregg: Oh, that. We had a phone conversation, Mr. Cigar and I. He promised me you'd be cool—not name any names. So long as the boy's identity is protected, I have no problem. I'm not angry. Besides, firing long arms in the street isn't exactly my style. I prefer a quieter, more civilized approach.

Hoag: Poison?

Gregg: (laughs) No. I'm really an old-fashioned sort of bloke at heart, Mr. Hoag. I hire lawyers. Quite dear ones.

(end tape)

* * *

(Tape #2 with Marco Bartucci. Recorded in his office at Jumbo's Disco Nov. 30. Hasn't licked his stubborn perspiration problem.)

Bartucci: Our second tour of the States was an entirely different story from the first. *More for Me* was the number one selling album there. At the very same time, their movie, *Rough Boys*, was the summer's hottest release, and it in turn had a hit soundtrack of its own. Ever see it, Mr. Hoag?

Hoag: Eight times in one weekend.

Bartucci: The kids screamed for them now like they had for the Beatles. They sold out Shea Stadium. Played the *Sullivan Show.* Three sold-out shows at the Hollywood Bowl. A monster tour I put together, not that I'm trying to pat myself on the back.

Hoag: Of course not.

Bartucci: In Chicago, I took them to Chess Studios, where they recorded some of their favorite R and B songs backed up by old-time Chicago bluesmen. *Chess Moves* it was called.

Hoag: How come it was never released in the U.S.?

Bartucci: The record company thought it would compete with the live album of the *More for Me* tour. The boys enjoyed the Chess sessions. They enjoyed the tour. Marco took care of everything for them. After the show, Jack filled their rooms with liquor and pot and fifteen or more game young ladies—innocent fun compared with what went on later, with the heroin, the sexual perversity, the wanton destruction of hotel property. Back then, they were merely fun-loving, horny boys. Touring was a tremendous release for them. Here at home there was great pressure on them to go into the studio and make more hits. There were also the domestic pressures. T. S. and Tulip had married. Secretly—EMI and I felt it was best that way. Here was this impudent stud, this bad-boy idol of millions. He just oughtn't be married to the famous daughter of a prominent barrister, especially one who took him to the ballet and taught him to eat with a knife and fork. It wasn't his image. It wasn't *him.* The second he got away from Tulip on tour, he rebelled with both hands. This made Rory happy. He preferred the old T. S. The old clubs, too. In the giant arenas, with all of the kids screaming, Rory said he was starting to feel like a performing monkey. One night, to prove a point, he stopped hitting the strings entirely. The kids were making so much noise they didn't even notice. *(laughs)* That tour was a gas. Until they lowered the boom on poor Puppy, of course.

Hoag: What happened exactly?

Bartucci: We should have stayed out of the South. But we'd gotten so much press there before . . . When we'd arrive in a city, the police and hotel management would get tipped off by me with regard to what type of party scene the boys might get themselves into—and how we certainly would appreciate it if this stayed quiet. They always cooperated. After all, the boys generated a lot of local revenue. I always carried a suitcase full of cash, as well. Never had a problem, until we got to Little Rock, Arkansas, where we encountered a particular police official who was not at all into the idea of some black musician getting white girls stoned and then balling them. This fellow was *not* going to look the other way, no matter how much money I offered him. Far from it—he wanted to make a statement. And he bloody well did. His men broke down the door to Puppy's hotel room at two a.m. and found him there in bed with a naked fifteen-year-old white girl, and in possession of hashish and amphetamines. And he was in some very, very deep shit, the poor boy. Statutory rape, they called it. The drug possession charge was no small matter either. The record company, Capitol, sent down a big-time New York attorney at once. I told the other boys to take off, but they refused. They were loyal, those three, I'll grant them that. The lawyer bargained and arm-twisted and somehow kept Puppy out of jail. He pleaded guilty to possession and to unlawful trafficking with a minor, or some such thing, in exchange for which he was fined ten thousand dollars and placed on probation for three years. We were elated—until Washington decided to get in on it. Your government was most displeased to discover Puppy was actually one of yours—it meant they couldn't make a point of kicking him out of the country. So they kicked the rest of us out. Revoked our work visas, and made it very clear that Us was no longer welcome in America, at least not if Puppy Johnson was in the band. So we came home. Toured the Continent. *Chess Moves* sold well here. And then that bloody psychedelic thing happened.

Hoag: They started dropping acid.

Bartucci: The Beatles, they flourished from LSD—gave the world *Sergeant Pepper.* Everyone else produced the worst kind of self-indulgent crap imaginable. The Stones, under the influence of acid, did *Their Satanic Majesties Request*, unquestionably their worst album. And Us, oh my, they got so very weird, those boys. Withdrew to their country retreats and blasted off into their own little worlds. T. S. went into what I call his T. S. Eliot stage. Started writing unbelievably wretched stream-of-consciousness lyrics. Poetry, they called it. Rory, he got obsessed with Irish folk ballads from olden times. Derek started collecting Victorian pornographic art, as well as slender blond boys. Puppy just got into being rather glazed. Surly as well. The product of all of this, when they finally went back into the studio, was *Rock of Ages*, which they called a musical exploration of their once and future selves.

Hoag: "Mystical vipers/Windscreen wipers/Across the twisting purple corridors/Inside our minds."

Bartucci: I called it crap. Christ, they expressed themselves musically as druids! Chanted! And their music of tomorrow—it was *noise.* Two entire cuts were *noise.* There wasn't one marketable single on it. Plus they took some very nasty shots at the royal family. The EMI people loathed it, fought with them every step of the way. *Rock of Ages* was a critical and commercial failure, here and abroad. Their first failure. But you couldn't tell the boys this accurately reflected its quality. Oh no. Their heads were too large. They actually blamed EMI for its failure—creative interference, they called it. So T. S. brought in Tulip's father to examine all of their contracts and financial affairs. He told them they should form their own label, which naturally appealed to their grandiose delusions. He also told them I was stealing from them. I wasn't, as I've made clear to you, but the more drugs they took, the more they believed him. T. S. still blames me for the tax troubles he got into—and I wasn't even around by then. They called me the vilest names, after all I did for them. Left me with no choice but to hire a solicitor of my own. We reached a settlement. Parted company. They went on to do some of their most successful work. But the truth is they were never happy again. Look what happened to them—heroin, divorce, death. There were no good times after that, Mr. Hoag. It gives me no pleasure to say so. I bear them no grudge. The hard feelings, those went away years ago . . . Anything else I can tell you? I'm rather busy.

Hoag: Just one thing: Where did you go after our interview on Friday?

Bartucci: Why do you ask?

Hoag: I was wondering if you happened to be around, say, Savile Row.

Bartucci: I was right here. Working.

Hoag: Can anyone here vouch for you?

Bartucci: Vouch for me?

Hoag: Yes. Do you mind if I ask some of them?

Bartucci: I most certainly do mind. Where I go and what I do is none of your or Tristam Scarr's damned business. And you can tell that cheap, phony bastard I said so!

Hoag: Sure there still isn't just the tiniest grudge?

Bartucci: I think you should leave, Mr. Hoag.

Hoag: I'll do that. Again, thank you for your time and your—

Bartucci: Get the fuck out of my—!

(end tape)

(Tape #1 with Tulip recorded in her Chelsea flat Dec. 1. Located on King's Road directly over a shop specializing in metal-studded collars and handcuffs. Parlor is messy. The Mod Bod weighs possibly fifty pounds more than in her heyday. Face is fleshy, blotchy. Hair uncombed and greasy. Wears large silver cross on chain around her neck. Holds Bible in her lap.)

Hoag: I've met your daughter Violet. Lovely girl.

Tulip: She's no longer mine. I've lost her. He's won.

Hoag: Do you mean Tris? *(silence)* So what are you doing with yourself these days?

Tulip: Do you mean now that I'm the Mod Blob?

Hoag: I mean now that you're not nineteen, and London doesn't swing like a pendulum do.

Tulip: I've a small family income. And I'm very active in my church.

Hoag: According to Tris it's not one of the more established faiths.

Tulip: It's so like him to condemn what he doesn't understand.

Hoag: Could we talk about when you first met him?

Tulip: I was thin, rich and beautiful. A spoiled little bitch as well. Anything I'd ever wanted I'd gotten. Us were the hot new group, very gear. I was at the Ad Lib one night with David Bailey and a few others. And so were the two of them, Tris and Rory. I'd heard what people were saying about them, that they chewed up pretty little girls and spit them out. Perhaps that attracted me. I don't know. I do know I thought it couldn't possibly happen to me. Not Tulip. It was Rory I got involved with first, actually. He was the sweetest, baddest little boy. Had this way of cocking his head to one side when he talked to me, as if he knew he was bad and couldn't help himself. And he *couldn't.* Rory was the first man I ever fell for, and I fell hard . . . And it all turned out to be true, what people had said. He *was* mean. He lied to me, slept around on me. S-So I started sleeping with Tris, to get back at him. Only I fell even harder for Tris. Sounds awful, doesn't it? I was an awful, drugged-out bitch. I was a slut.

Hoag: You were his wife.

Tulip: Yes, I was. And by the time that became public I was sleeping with Rory once again, God help me, and poor Derek was wishing *he* was. Madness, all of it. A loss of self-control brought on by abandoning the Lord and his teachings.

Hoag: What was it like being secretly married?

Tulip: I despised it. Ours was a proper marriage—for a while, at least—but the newspapers made me out to be some kind of rock 'n' roll tramp. And I had to take it. He had his bloody image to maintain.

Hoag: Derek thinks you're the only person who ever really got to know Tris.

Tulip: (pause) Tris was . . . is . . . a vulnerable person. Shy, actually. Whatever came out of him, whether it was meanness or genius, came from this well of insecurity. As a result, I could never hate him, even when I wanted to. He never did learn how to feel comfortable with people. They in turn never wanted to understand him. When I met him he was twenty-two.

The music he made, the life he led—it was all totally new. What he came to resent, I think, was that everyone wanted him to stay the same angry boy making the same angry music. They wouldn't allow him to grow as an artist or as a person. He was, for example, very excited and fulfilled by *Rock of Ages.* Until people totally rejected it . . . Our life together was a fairy tale. We were lovely, special little children who could buy all the toys and candy we wanted, and there were no adults around to slap our hands and tell us no. They bought these lovely *Alice in Wonderland* cottages in the Cotswolds, and filled them with toys and animals. Tris had an elephant, a giraffe, an entire zoo of his own, just like Dr. Dolittle, until he decided one night it was cruel and set them free. The village was not pleased . . . London wasn't fun anymore. Fans would hassle us. Jack would drive us in sometimes for a night out, but mostly we stayed in the country. We all had cooks, and there were always lovely people around. George and Patti Harrison, Eric, Keith, Brian, Woody. All the mates. Lots of girls. Lots of jams. Lots of magic mushrooms, mescaline, THC . . .

Hoag: What kind of relationship did you have with Puppy?

Tulip: Puppy thought I was some kind of evil witch, bad for Tris and Rory's heads, bad for the band. He was forever mean to me. And then after the ban he was just mean to everyone. Puppy didn't care for the country life. He only came out when they got together to play. Usually he'd crash at Rory's, where all of the equipment was.

Hoag: Like the weekend he died?

Tulip: Yes. Like the weekend he died.

Hoag: Can you tell me about that?

Tulip: It was after *Rock of Ages* flopped. Tris and Rory were taking it very hard. They felt personally betrayed by the fans and the critics. Puppy blamed himself for them not being able to give it American tour support. The weekend he died they'd gotten together at Rory's to talk about their next album. They were not getting far. I think their faith in each other had been shaken. It was frightening, the amount of pressure that was put on them by Marco, by EMI, by the good new groups—Cream, Traffic, Procol Harem. There was no laughter in Rory's house that weekend. No joy. I remember this girl he was seeing then, she picked right up on that.

Hoag: The tarot card woman?

Tulip: Yes. That's right.

Hoag: Do you remember her name?

Tulip: (pause) No. She was just some girl. Rory didn't see her for long. He didn't see anyone for long . . . They were in the music room, trying out some things, drinking some champagne, talking. Marco had just left to go back to London.

Hoag: What was Marco doing there?

Tulip: Hassling them, mostly. Jack and I were out in the kitchen with a few other girls and friends. They didn't like for us to be in there with them when they were in the early stages. I remember there was an argument. Rory said something like, "Fuck this flower-power shit!" Then there was this terrible crash. Derek came rushing out, terribly pale, and said "Jackie, Pup has passed out and we can't bring him to." We all went in and found him collapsed amidst his drums. Jack tried to revive him while the rest of us looked for whatever it was he'd taken.

Hoag: You didn't find anything.

Tulip: No. The pills weren't to be found. By the time the ambulance arrived, he was gone. The Lord had taken him from us.

Hoag: Do you think someone acted as His agent?

Tulip: Agent?

Hoag: Tris thinks Puppy was murdered by one of you.

Tulip: We were all to blame.

Hoag: You were?

Tulip: He died for our sins. That's why the Lord took him. To punish us. To *warn* us. But we didn't heed His message. We were too blind. So things got worse. More drugs, more pain, more death . . . Us wasn't the same after Puppy died. They used studio drummers from then on, none with his talent or flair. The focus shifted more to Tris and Rory. *We're Double Trouble*, the album they turned out after Puppy's death, was shit-kicking, wired rock 'n' roll. They'd put away the hollow-body blues. The acid as well. From then on it was coke, smack, speed, all of the above. We three became serious smack freaks. I was getting it on with both of them then, God help me.

Hoag: How did they handle that? Didn't they fight over you?

Tulip: Never. Deep down, they always meant more to each other than any woman could.

Hoag: Even you?

Tulip: Especially me . . . Their new sound clicked. They bounced back bigger than ever, and started acting like genuine bad-ass stars. Pissing people off. Getting shit-faced and disorderly in public. Seeing what they could get away with—just like two bad little boys. And when they toured, forget it. I tried going with them on their return tour to America in '68. It was male macho madness. They trashed their hotel rooms with fire hoses. Threw the furniture in the street. One night in Detroit Rory got in a brawl with the hotel manager because they wanted to put him on the second floor. I said to him "So what?" He said, "It's no bleedin' fun to dangle a groupie out of a second-story window." In Kansas City, I came in one morning and found Tris in *our* bed with two girls and someone's pet monkey. I split. I couldn't take it. The following year, when they went over to tour promote *Skullduggery*, Rory asked me to go with them. I didn't want to but he begged me. So I traveled as Tris's wife on the tour, while I was actually living with Rory. It was sick, sick, sick . . . My friends were always asking me which of them was better in bed. I always said it was like comparing coke with smack—they were both obscenely great and it was impossible to say which would kill you faster. At least Rory didn't beat me.

Hoag: Tris beat you?

Tulip: Tris was often violent when he was on smack. Broke my nose once. *Skullduggery* stayed at number one for something like five months. Then they put out *Nasty, Nasty*, and it was nearly as big. That's when they had to cool out somewhere for tax reasons.

Hoag: Tris moved to L.A.

Tulip: And Rory and Derek to Italy. I stayed here and tried to get myself somewhat back together. Got off drugs. Went to Italy and got off Rory. Then I flew to L.A. to see Tris. He was living in a rented mansion in Malibu, and much, much closer to the edge. Shooting up. Drinking too much tequila. Hanging out with problem children like Moon, and Dennis Wilson of the Beach Boys. Dennis he'd gotten to be friendly with after the '68 tour, when Dennis was living on Sunset. Both of those two are dead now. The night before I got there the police caught Tris going a hundred and fifty miles per hour on Pacific Coast Highway in his Porsche—with a suspended license. I had to bail him out of jail. He'd changed for the worse. He was so absolutely full of anger. Hate.

Hoag: Do you know why?

Tulip: You'd have to ask him. He wouldn't open up to me. That's why I left him—that and the smack. It wasn't until Jack and Derek moved out there and got hold of him that he started getting himself together again. When he did, I took him back. Had Violet. Then we split again, for good . . . All of it's such a blur now. I can't even remember most of the faces. I have my photo album, of course, but I haven't been able to look at that for years now. Freaks me out too much. I took a lot of the pictures myself, actually.

Hoag: I'd love to see it.

Tulip: I actually fancied I'd be a photographer one day. David Bailey said I was quite good. I never followed through, though. Never followed through on anything, except falling apart. If I hadn't found the Lord, I'd be dead just like Rory. Poor, poor Rory . . .

Hoag: I really would love to see it.

Tulip: Hmm? Oh, it's somewhere . . . I had to put it away when I found Violet pawing through it. Pawing through my past. I'll dig it up for you. Come back tomorrow.

Hoag: Thank you. I will.

Tulip: All I ever did was model. Not that that's anything. You're just a slab of beef.

Hoag: How do you feel about Violet following in your footsteps?

Tulip: It's her life.

Hoag: And T. S.?

Tulip: What about him?

Hoag: How do you feel about him?

Tulip: I don't feel anything about him anymore.

(end tape)

CHAPTER EIGHT

Lulu was getting soft.

Too much of Merilee's cooking and too little physical activity had dulled her razor-sharp huntress instincts. She was slow to react when I let myself into the mews house. In fact, she didn't react at all.

I knelt and scratched her ears. She sniffed at my fingers with the cool reserve she usually shows roach exterminators and federal census takers. I hadn't visited her on her bed of pain for two whole days. I was getting the treatment for it.

"This has gone far enough," I told her firmly. "I've already apologized numerous times for what happened. And you *know* I can't be here with you all the time."

I reached down to hoist her out of her bed. She resisted me, grunting unappreciatively. I'm bigger. I lifted her up and held her. Usually, she likes to nestle into me and put her head on my shoulder like a dance partner. Not now. Now she squirmed in my arms, and wanted to be put down. I obliged her.

"Okay, be a martyr," I said, as I headed for the phone. "See what it gets you."

Tris was still asleep and not taking any calls. I told Pamela I'd be late for work the next evening because I wanted to look through Tulip's photo album. She said she'd pass the news on to Mr. Scarr. She also said she'd quite enjoyed transcribing our last couple of tapes.

"I really do hear him now, Hoagy."

"Glad you think so," I said, pleased she'd noticed a difference. I *was* getting him now. If only I was getting closer to figuring out who'd shot at me, too. Then I'd be making real progress.

I had just enough time to soak in a hot tub with a Laphroaig—it *wasn't* too smoky for me—before it was time to watch part ten of *Giant Worms of the Sea.* I was very into this series now I wasn't sure why. Two possibilities came to mind. Either it was an acquired taste or I'd been in England too long.

When the show was over, I put my new suit on over a black cashmere turtleneck and spooned out a can of mackerel for Lulu. She glowered at it like it was Alpo beef chunks. Still, I said good-bye fondly, hoping she'd feel guilty over the way she'd been treating me. I'm sure she didn't.

The mini was still out of service, so I was using the Peugeot diesel wagon. It went from zero to sixty in a day and a half, and had no fridge, but driving it made me nostalgic. I'd had a diesel just like it the year I lived in the Perigord Valley, subsisting on goose liver pâté and chilled Monbazillac while I struggled with the first draft of *Our Family Enterprise.* Ah, youth.

I parked near the theater and waited for Merilee at the performer's entrance like a stage-door Johnny, flowers and all. A dapper older gent was also waiting there for a cast member, though I think it likely the fluffy blond object of his affections was named Steve.

She came out wearing her long, treasured Perry Ellis tweed suit—she'd wept when he died. A high-throated white silk blouse, alligator belt and shoes went with it. Her eyes got soft when I handed her the flowers.

Fans at the curb pushed autograph books at her. Flashbulbs popped. It was, possibly, indiscreet for the two of us to be seen together like this. But we'd decided it would be tawdry if we behaved like we had something to hide. We had never been tawdry, and didn't intend to start now

"How's T. S.?" she asked, as I steered her toward the car.

"I'm actually starting to respect him a little," I replied. "Not that he's a very nice guy—guys who make a commitment to being the best seldom are. He knows he hurt people. But he was willing to pay that price. You don't meet many people anymore who care that much about their art. *And* have talent."

She squeezed my arm. "Ever think you'd find yourself identifying with a rock star?"

"Who's identifying with a rock star?"

"Sorry, darling. I must have misunderstood."

Merilee had something on her mind. She sat with her back stiff as we rode to the restaurant, and kept wringing her hands in her lap. I kept up a line of polite chatter and waited her out. I waited a long time. She held it in all the way to the Grange, which is a very fine eating place on King Street in Covent Garden. She held it in through the martinis, complete with extra olives. She held it in while we destroyed their beef Wellington and two of their most amusing bottles of Haut-Médoc. It was only after the table had been cleared and the coffee poured that she spilled it:

"Zack wants to come over."

I tugged at my ear. "For how long?"

"A-A few days. He said he feels like we're drifting apart. He wants to—"

"Have it out?"

"No. I don't think so."

"Any idea when he's planning to come?"

She swallowed and examined her coffee cup. "Tomorrow afternoon."

I pushed my coffee away and called for a Calvados. Then I took a deep breath and let it out slowly.

"Sometimes," she offered, "things aren't as neat as one would like."

"Things are never that neat."

"Zack is my husband, darling. While he's in London he expects me to be his wife."

"And what do you expect?"

"I expect nothing anymore," she replied bitterly. "I feel like a cigarette."

"You don't smoke. You've never smoked."

"You're right. I'm being actressy. Sorry." She swept her hair back. "I'm going to be a good wife to him while he's here. I'm going to be the best damned wife I know how to be, even though I am being torn apart at the seams. And I'm very, very sorry about this. For you and for me. I've been so happy the past few—"

"Don't. Don't be sorry. I'll take my things with me in the morning. Call me when you can, okay?"

She looked at me quizzically. "You're being awfully damned understanding."

"You were once very understanding."

Her glance flickered south of my equator. "I tried to be."

I drained my Calvados. "Good thing I've got the station wagon. I can put Lulu right in the back, bed and all."

Merilee cleared her throat uncomfortably. "I still think she should stay with me."

"Merilee, she's my dog—even if she doesn't happen to be speaking to me right now."

"She's *our* dog."

"She's *my* dog. I told you before—we're a package. If I go, she goes with me."

"I know, I know. Only, I still think she's safer with me."

"No."

"You may still be in danger."

"No!"

"You could stop by anytime and visit her. Keep the key."

"Merilee, you're asking me to give her up."

"Just temporarily." She put her hand over mine. "I need her, darling. Don't you see? If she's there, you're there. Holding on to her is the only way I'll make it through this. Please, darling. Please?"

It's a good thing Merilee Nash doesn't have a diabolical nature. I'd assassinate a head of state for her, if she asked me like that. "And what about afterward?"

"We agreed we wouldn't talk about afterward."

"To hell with what we agreed, Merilee."

"Very well. What do you want?"

"I think that's pretty obvious."

"Try making it a little more obvious, if you don't mind."

"I don't mind. What happens at the end of *The Philadelphia Story*?"

"The curtain comes down."

"Before that."

Merilee flushed. "I-I get married to my first husband again."

"Suggest anything to you?"

She sighed. "Happy endings are for plays, darling. And very, very old ones at that."

"I kind of like happy endings."

"I always thought you preferred the tragic, deep kind."

"Not when I'm in the cast."

Her forehead creased. It does that when she's trying not to cry. "God, you look good in black, Mr. Hoagy."

"You look good in everything, but I suppose you already know that."

"A gal only knows it if her guy says so."

"Am I your guy?"

"I wish I knew, darling," she said softly. "I'm so sorry."

"Don't be." I cupped her chin in my palm and got lost in her green eyes for a second. "You're still mine for one more night."

London's vacant-stare district that season was King's Road, Chelsea. Zonked, translucent punks shuffled along the sidewalk in black leather, their hair dyed a spectrum of repulsive colors. The wandering victims. They looked like they had framed eight-by-ten glossies of Sid Vicious hanging over their beds of nails.

I still didn't know whether punk was a posture or a statement. More important, I didn't care. I had enough problems of my own. I'd just said good-bye to Merilee and to Lulu, and I didn't know when I'd see either one of them again. The Irish oatmeal Merilee had made me eat before I left still sat in my stomach like a bucket of ready-mixed joint compound. My head ached.

I left the Peugeot at the curb outside of Tulip's building. I was about to buzz her flat when I noticed the street door had been jimmied open with a pry bar. The frame was smashed and splintered, the door ajar. I looked around. No one on the street seemed to be paying any attention to the ruined door, or to me, or to anything. I went in.

Tulip's flat was on the second floor in the front, and her hall door matched the one downstairs. Splintered and open. I hesitated there at the top of the stairs. This looked like a job for somebody else. Somebody with guts and a pit bull.

I listened at her door, mouth dry. My heart started to pound.

Silence. I knocked and called out her name. More silence. I took a deep breath. Then I pushed open the door and went in.

The closet in her entry hall had been ransacked. Its contents—scarves, shoulder bags, an old fringe buckskin jacket, an even older clear plastic rain slicker adorned with psychedelic flowers—were scattered on the floor.

I called out her name.

There had been a television and a cheap stereo sitting in a wall unit in the dingy parlor. They were gone now. Their outline remained in the dust there on the bare shelves. Lots of dust. I couldn't imagine what it looked like under her bed. I hoped I wouldn't have to find out.

I called out her name.

Dresser drawers had been yanked open in the bedroom. Underwear, socks, T-shirts were strewn everywhere. The jewelry box on her dressing table had been emptied and overturned. The bedroom closet had been tossed.

Dresses were heaped on the floor, shoe boxes dumped open upon them.

I called out her name.

The medicine chest over the bathroom sink had been pawed through. Open pill bottles were scattered in the sink, their contents dissolving in brightly colored smears under the dripping tap.

I called out her name.

Then I turned and banged into her.

Tulip was standing right there behind me in the doorway to the kitchen, her still-beautiful eyes open very wide, her face pale. She was pointing in the general direction of the parlor, and she was trying to say something to me but there was this unfortunate matter of the boning knife that someone had plunged into her stomach. All she could get out was a gurgling noise as she staggered toward me. I started to reach for her but not before she pitched forward into me. She was not a feather. We both went down, she directly on top of me—and if you think that doesn't still give me nightmares, guess again. I pushed her off of me and over onto her back as gently as I could. But there was no need for me to be gentle. She was dead now.

Whoever did it to her had been thorough. He'd taken the silver cross from around her neck, too.

The British press handled the murder of Tulip, the once-famous Mod Bod, as a kind of sad postscript to the sixties and Swinging London. Her old glamour shots were pulled out and splashed over the front pages, along with the recollections of those who'd been there. Or claimed to have been there. A revolution, Derek had called it. The staid newspapers indulged in sober discussion of the early burnout and death that had overtaken so many of the youthful Carnaby Street luminaries—Brian, Puppy, Hendrix, Moon. The tabloids went straight for the low road, with gleeful stories about her weight, and how it had ballooned. Stories about how shed taken to spending her time at a storefront halfway-house mission called the Church of Life. Stories about how she'd lived, and died, in total squalor.

I was there. It wasn't squalor. But it didn't swing, either.

Jay Weintraub released a brief statement to the press on Tristam Scarr's behalf: "Tulip was the only woman I have ever loved. She was the mother of my only child. Although we spent our lives apart in recent years, our feelings for each other never changed. I will always love her, and miss her terribly."

It was the only comment on her murder that T. S. made, and he didn't make it. He was in no shape to do so. Her death had so severely jolted him that a doctor was keeping him sedated.

The statement came from me. All a part of the service. Just

don't ask me to do thank-you notes or windows. I get a little crabby.

Our editor phoned from New York to make sure I was on top of this sizzling new development. I assured him I was, right down to the bloodstains all over my trenchcoat. *Rolling Stone*, he disclosed, would pay dearly for my exclusive first-person account. It would, he suggested, give the book "monster topspin." I said it was a great idea. I lied. I had no intention of exploiting Tulip's death. But editors feel better about themselves and you if they think you agree with their suggestions. Especially editors who use words like "topspin."

By all the press accounts, Tulip had walked in on a burglary taking place in her flat, and had gotten killed for it. Whatever she owned of value had been taken. The ransacking of the drugs in her medicine chest suggested that her murderer was an addict.

The police, however, had a problem with this theory. I learned about it from Farley Root, that same apologetic buck-toothed, redheaded investigator in that same nile green suit. He made the trip out to Gadpole two mornings later, joined by a strapping uniformed officer who didn't speak. The three of us sat around the kitchen table. Pamela put on tea.

"Nice to see you again, Inspector," I said.

"It's kind of you to say so, Mr. Hoag."

"Hoagy," I said.

"Hoagy. Right. And while we're at it, I'm not actually an—"

"Your neck looks much better. Try that talc?"

Root reddened, glanced self-consciously over at the uniformed officer, who was working hard at not smirking. "I did," he replied. "Floris number eighty-nine. Very soothing, as you suggested. Thank you."

"My pleasure."

Pamela served us our tea as well as some hot scones. Then

she returned to the laundry room, where she was in the process of removing the bloodstains from my trench coat. Don't ask me how. I never press the masters for their secrets.

"Turn up any of those bullets yet?" I asked Root.

He bit into a scone, driving his long front teeth into it like a gopher. "No sir, we haven't," he replied, gnawing. "But that brings me to my business—Miss Tulip's murder. It does seem rather straightforward on *the* surface. She returns home, discovers someone there in the act, and there we have it. Unfortunate timing. Break-ins are rather common in that district. Several have taken place in recent weeks, though none with so grievous an outcome."

I sipped my tea and waited him out.

"I can find only one flaw in this reasoning," Root said.

"Which is. . . ?"

"You, sir."

"Me?"

"Yessir. I don't wish to jump to erroneous conclusions, but this is the second bit of ugly business you've been party to in the past several days. I was inclined to classify the first incident as random street violence, and you as the victim of a bit of bad luck. But I'm afraid with this second incident . . . Well, you can see my point, can't you?"

I tugged at my ear. "Yes, I believe I can."

"Glad to hear that," Root said, pleased. "Now then, Hoagy can you account for how you've found yourself at the scene of two violent attacks recently?"

"No, I can't."

Root stared at me, visibly disappointed by my answer. "I see," he said at last. "You told the officers at the murder scene you had an appointment with Miss Tulip. What exactly was your business?"

"As I told you before, I'm helping Tris Scarr do his memoirs."

Root asked me for the name of the publisher. I gave him topspin's name. Then he told me to continue.

"Tulip played a big part in his life," I said. "I'd met with her in reference to that. And I was supposed to meet with her again."

"How did she seem to you?"

"Seem?"

"Her state of mind."

"About as messed up as the rest of us. Maybe a little more."

Root nodded. "Any idea what sort of people she knew?"

"Not really. She did tell me she was involved with her church."

Root glanced through his notepad. "Yes. Fellow who operates it, called Father Bob, used to deal drugs. Been to jail for it, actually. There's also some question as to the validity of his divinity school training."

"Think he might be involved in it somehow?"

"No, I think you are, Hoagy," Root said evenly.

He watched me for a reaction from across the table, bony, freckled hands folded in front of him, eyes impassive. Bashful he wasn't, not when he felt he was being shut out.

I cleared my throat. "I appreciate your candor, Inspector."

"I place great stock in candor. And I'm *not* actually an—"

"And I do understand how you feel. I wish I had an explanation for what's been happening to me. Around me. But I don't. I'm sorry."

"As am I."

"I will make a deal with you, though."

Root glanced over at his uniformed colleague, then back at me. "A deal?"

"Yes. If I do come up with something, I'll share it with you—if you'll share something with me now."

"I don't make deals such as those, sir," Root said firmly.

"Too bad."

He swallowed, craned his neck. "Share what with you?"

"Have you inventoried the contents of Tulip's apartment?"

Root turned to the other officer, who nodded.

"Could I get a copy of the inventory?" I asked.

Root frowned. "For what reason?"

"Let's put it this way—I need it."

He thought it over carefully. "Very well. You shall have it," he said, draining his tea.

Pamela appeared instantly from the laundry room. "More tea, Inspector?"

"No thank you, madam," he replied. "And I'm *not* an—"

"Another scone, perhaps?" she said.

"Thank you. No. But I would appreciate a word with Mr. Scarr, if that's possible."

She shook her head. "I'm afraid it isn't. Mr. Scarr wasn't strong to begin with, and the loss of Tulip has quite simply devastated him. The doctor insisted he not be disturbed."

"Of course. Terribly sorry. Didn't mean to seem insensitive." Root lurched to his feet. "We'll be going then."

I showed them out, past the guards on the front door, and the surveillance cameras and the floodlights.

"Certainly believes in security, doesn't he?" observed Root, as he climbed into his unmarked Austin Metro.

"He believes in feeling safe," I said. "Can't say I blame him."

Root rolled down his window, stuck his head out, "One more question, Hoagy."

"Yes?"

"What is a cheese steak?"

"A hero sandwich—thin strips of steak topped with sautéed onions, mushrooms, and melted cheese."

"Good Lord, sounds wonderful."

"If you want a good one you have to go to Philadelphia. The Liberty Bell is there. It's not the worst place there is."

"Can't say I'll be getting to Philadelphia soon."

"Neither will W. C. Fields."

Tris looked different to me. Partly it was his hair. Pamela, that woman of many talents, had trimmed it for him. But mostly, I realized, I'd Just never seen him in the daylight before. He looked even more cadaverous and ghoulish than he did in his dimly lit royal chamber. Flesh-toned he was not.

He and I rode together in the back seat of the Silver Cloud to Tulip's funeral, which was at her church in London. He wore a chalk-striped navy blue suit, white shirt, dark striped tie, ankle boots, and the look of a lost, bewildered little boy. Jack and Violet were up front, Jack behind the wheel with his jaw set grimly. Violet had on a black dress. Her luxuriant black hair was tied tightly back, and she was sniffling. For the first time since I'd met her, she looked her age.

Four bodyguards rode in the car ahead of us.

"I intended to thank you, Hogarth," Tris said softly.

"For what?"

"The statement you wrote. It was very sensitive. I couldn't have said it so well myself."

"Sure you could have. You just needed a little time to recover."

He dragged deeply on a Gauloise, let the smoke out of his famous flaring nostrils. "Thank you. I mean it."

"Forget it. We ear-wigglers have to stick together."

"That we do." He gazed out the window. "It's true, Hogarth."

"What's true?"

"What Derek said—I have no mates. Not true ones. Not anymore. I-I don't make 'em easily, and when I do, I make 'em for life. I make 'em for forever . . . It's not as if she's gone. Or

Rory's gone. They're in here." He tapped his head with his finger. "They're still in here."

"I understand."

"Do you, mate?"

"Sure. I'm the same way."

He smiled at me. I smiled back. Inwardly, I sighed. It was happening—he and I were getting emotionally involved. It was only natural. I'd gotten him to open up, share his secrets, his dreams, his hurts with me. That didn't happen without feelings happening, too. From both directions. I didn't know to do it any other way. How did the lunch-pail ghosts do it? I wondered. No, I didn't. I didn't ever want to know that.

Tris punched the leather seat between us hard with his fist. "Damn them!"

"Damn who?"

"The fates. I mean, why Tulip? Why *her*?"

I glanced over at him. Quietly I said, "It wasn't the fates, Tristam."

He narrowed his pouched eyes at me. Then he reached for a button on the door panel next to him, and said, "Excuse us for a moment, people." The glass divider to the front seat slid shut. Jack and Violet couldn't hear us now. "What are you talking about, Hogarth? What is this?"

"It's trouble."

"What sort of trouble?"

"That break-in wasn't what it appeared to be. The use of the pry bar, the theft of the valuables, the ransacking of the medicine chest—all that was just done to cover up what really happened."

"Which was?"

"Which was that somebody Tulip knew dropped by to visit her, and kill her, and take something. Something that was very valuable to them, but not to anybody else."

"Such as what?"

"Her photo album. I saw the police inventory of the apartment contents this morning. No photo album. It's gone."

He put out his cigarette and lit another. "Right . . . Pammy said you'd phoned, and were planning to go see this album of Tu's." He scratched his head. "Can't seem to recall anything about it though."

"She took pictures."

He let out a short laugh. "That I recall. Always in m'face with her bleedin' Nikon camera, she was."

"And she kept them. Pictures of you guys on tour, on stage, at home. Pictures of London, pictures of Paris, New York, L.A., everywhere."

An odd look flickered across his face, like he'd just taken a pan of ice water down his pants. It was gone in an instant.

"There must have been a photo in the album that I couldn't be allowed to see," I went on. "A photo that would have told me who killed Puppy, and who shot at me. But it's gone now, and so is she. She must have been able to tie it all together. That's why she had to die. Now we'll never—" I stopped myself short. "Unless . . ."

"Unless what, Hogarth?"

"Nothing. Just a thought."

"You've told the police all of this?"

"No. Not yet."

"Why not? It seems to me they—"

"It's part of the past. Your past. That's not their area. It's mine."

He grinned at me crookedly. "And you're still bleedin' mad about your dog getting shot."

"And I'm still bleedin' mad about my dog getting shot."

At least she used to be my dog. I wasn't so sure anymore. I

was still waiting to hear from Merilee. And trying not to think about her and Zack.

Tris put his hand on my arm. "Who is it, Hogarth? Who's doing these things?"

"I don't know yet."

I had ideas though. Plenty. I'd asked Pamela if she'd told anybody besides Tris that I'd be checking out Tulip's album. She had. She'd told Jack—the very same Jack who, once again, was away from Gadpole running errands when a certain violent shooting incident was taking place. There was no question that Jack looked mighty fine for it. After all, he had the biggest personal ax to grind against Puppy. He had shown the most resistance to talking about the past with me. He was good with a shotgun. And there was his relationship with Violet to consider. Maybe she was somehow involved in it with him. She did like to shoot. And to steal. Yeah, Jack looked mighty fine. But he wasn't the only one. The others could have known I was going to look at Tulip's album. Tulip could have mentioned it to them herself. Told Derek. Told Marco. It could have been one of them. It could have been any of them.

Yeah, I had ideas. Too many.

The Church of Life was housed in a shabby storefront down the street from Tulip's flat. Boisterous reporters, photographers, and TV cameramen were crowded onto the sidewalk and into the street out front, waiting anxiously for this rare public glimpse of the great T. S. He put on a pair of cool-cat wraparound shades when we pulled up. Then he tensed and took a deep breath. Jack jumped out first and opened his door for him.

They barraged him with questions the instant we stepped out of the Rolls. T. S. answered none of them. He had already made his one statement. His phalanx of guards somehow cleared a path through the crowd and we headed inside, T. S. with his arm protectively around Violet, who was about six inches taller than he in her heels.

Inside, the Church of Life looked a lot like a Bowery soup kitchen. There were long, scarred tables with benches on either side, a coffee urn, a bulletin board, the pungent smell of commercial disinfectant. Derek Gregg and Marco Bartucci, the human teapot, sat across from each other at one of the tables. No one else had come to see the Mod Bod off. Her parents were dead. The press were kept out.

At the far end of the room was a pulpit, where Father Bob presided. Father Bob had eaten fried eggs for breakfast that morning. Some of the yolk was still in his beard, which was black and bushy. He wore wire-rimmed glasses, a paint-splattered gray sweatshirt with the sleeves cut crudely off at the elbows, and rumpled black corduroy trousers. Thick black hair sprouted on his arms and up from under the neck of his sweatshirt, nearly meeting his beard.

The urn holding Tulip's ashes was on the table next to him.

The funeral service was short and casual. Just a few comments from Father Bob on how we all touch each other in life and in death. Then he presented Vi with the urn, and kissed her on the forehead.

T. S. exchanged a few words and a hug with Derek—and, after a hesitation, one with Marco, who was weeping openly. Then he headed back out to the car. Jack also hugged Derek. But the former Rough Boys drummer steered carefully around Marco. Marco noticed. I noticed. Marco noticed I noticed.

"Awful business, Mr. Hoag," Marco said, coming over to me. "Awful."

"Indeed," I said. "Had you seen her recently? Spoken to her?"

Marco frowned. "Why, no. Why do you ask?"

"Just wondered if the two of you were close."

"One needn't be in regular touch to be close. She was the loveliest of them all, Mr. Hoag. She was so lovely she could break your heart—without even trying." Marco ducked his head and swiped at his nose. Then he waddled out.

I watched him go, wondering just how long he had carried the torch for Tulip, and if he had ever tried doing anything about it, the poor, greasy little crook.

Tris was slouched in the back seat of the Silver Cloud, staring out the window. He stayed that way as we worked our way out of London. Then he sat up abruptly, opened the portable bar, and poured himself a brandy. His hands shook so badly he dribbled most of it onto the carpet. I grabbed the decanter from him and filled his glass. He took it all down in one gulp, then fell back against the seat, a hint of color in his cheeks now.

"All dead," he said hoarsely. "All dead."

I poured a brandy for myself.

"I'm the only one left, Hogarth. I'm next. Don't you see? I go next."

"You're right. You do."

He glared at me. "That's bloody reassuring of you, mate," he snarled.

"We all go next, Tristam. We're all headed in the same direction. No getting around it. Just do me one favor."

"What's that, Hogarth?"

"Hang out for a little while longer—I'm not done with you yet."

He let out a short harsh laugh and held out his empty glass.

I filled it for him. We killed the brandy together. By the time we rolled into Gadpole we were singing the refrain of "More for Me" together. He sounded a lot better on the album. I sounded great.

CHAPTER NINE

(Tape #7 with Tristam Scarr recorded in his chamber Dec. 7.)

Hoag: Tulip mentioned that something was bothering you when you lived in Los Angeles.

Scarr: What did she say about it?

Hoag: That you were restless, angry self-destructive. And that when she tried to get you to open up to her you—

Scarr: Beat the living shit out of her one night. Broke her nose and a couple of her front teeth. Next morning I didn't even remember it happening. That's how bombed I was getting, Hogarth. She kept getting real on me. Hassling me about Lord Harry. Hassling me about trashing m'life. All for m'own good, of course, but no one could tell me nothing then. She left me after that night. Went back to London. We got back together again when I got straight. She was eight months preggers at the time. Hadn't told me about that. A bit of a shock. We stayed together for another year or so, until it was over for good . . . To answer your question, a lot was bothering me in L.A. I was thirty years old and I was still acting sixteen. The whole T. S. bit was stale. I was tired of the music, the image, the road, Rory. I wanted to grow up. But I didn't know *how.*

Hoag: Who does? We're all faking it.

Scarr: I realize that now, but I didn't then. I just knew I didn't want to be T. S. anymore, and didn't know who I wanted to be instead. So I got angry. I got high. I copped out—blamed the fans for locking me into that image. Blamed the record company. Blamed Rory. Blamed everybody but m'self.

Hoag: You were still on top, weren't you?

Scarr: Yes, but our time was passing. The sixties were over. New bands with new sounds were coming along—Electric Light Orchestra, Genesis, Yes, Bowie, Roxy Music. We weren't on the cutting edge anymore. None of us were, really. Christ, McCartney was scoring a bleedin' James Bond movie. I thought Rory was holding me back. Rory thought I was holding him back. We stopped communicating. Started saying things about each other in the papers we didn't mean. And sometimes didn't even say, actually—you know how they are. He called me a manipulative swine. I called him a cockney lout. We were hurting inside, both of us. But we couldn't deal with it maturely, like brothers. So we split up. He went off to Italy. Did his solo album, *Bad Boy.*

Hoag: How did you feel when it became a hit?

Scarr: I was happy for him. Don't you see, Hogarth? There was no rivalry between us. The press made out that there was, so they could sell their papers. But there wasn't. Each of us needed to grow a bit. To do that, we needed to be apart. I needed to be *me.* The problem was that *me* was shards of broken glass.

Hoag: How much did the drugs have to do with that?

Scarr: (pause) I did a lot of 'em, and had a lot of good times doing 'em. Acid opened up my mind. I've no regrets about taking it, or smoking what I smoked. Coke and Lord Harry are another matter. They can take you over, especially if your life happens to be fucked up at that particular time. I got plain strung out on Lord Harry in L.A. And then it became the problem.

Hoag: Tulip said you were running with a pretty wild set of mates—Keith Moon, Dennis Wilson . . .

Scarr: Dennis who?

Hoag: Dennis Wilson of the Beach Boys.

Scarr: (pause) Oh, him. Yes, I recall him now. But we were never mates. She is . . . was mistaken about that. Just a bloke I got bombed with a few times. I was bombed all of the time, you see. I didn't want to be conscious. Things looked too much like shit when I was. So I basically tried to obliterate m'self on Lord Harry and women who'd let me do astonishingly cruel things to them. There were a number of them after Tulip left me, mostly would-be actresses who looked magnificent in bikinis, and out of them as well. I used them. They used me. Got their pictures in the paper when I was getting thrown out of Gazzarri's or Ciro's for being an abusive swine. Moon lived down the beach from me. Lennon was around for a bit as well. I believe Yoko had thrown him out. We three used to go out and raise decadent, drugged-out hell together.

Hoag: Were you doing anything musically—growing as you wanted to?

Scarr: I did a few country blues things in the studio with Phil Spector that I rather liked. Ry Cooder played guitar. I played m'harp. Whoever was around sat in—Bonnie Raitt, Stevie Stills, Lennon, Moon. Like a party, it was. But I had to be put in the hospital before I could get an album together, which I regretted. Only the one single, "Lucy Goosey," ever got released.

Hoag: Why were you hospitalized?

Scarr: Ulcers, the bleedin' sort. M'body was telling me to slow down, or I'd crash. Derek and Jack came out and took charge of me. Got me out of L.A. to the desert somewhere. Rented me a house with a pool and a full-time doctor. Saved m'life.

Hoag: You kicked?

Scarr: I did. Started eating proper. Swimming twice a day. Took nothing stronger than a glass of wine. And they got me talking to Rory again on the telephone. He'd cleaned up his own act as well. Was a sort of bleedin' jetsetter now—summers on the Riviera, winters skiing in Gstaad. Even had a live-in steady, a teenage Italian actress named Monica, who didn't shave under her arms . . . Christ, it was fantastic talking to Rory again. He was my *brother*, y'know? I think that was one of my biggest problems in L.A., my being away from Rory. We rang each other every night. Talked and talked about what had been going on between us. And when I was fit enough, I went and stayed with him at his place on the Riviera. We both broke down and cried like babies when I got out of the taxi . . . We wanted to play together again. We were ready. But only if it could be like it used to be, before the star-tripping and the bullshit.

Hoag: This is how the Johnny Thunder thing came about.

Scarr: That's right. It started as a sort of goof, y'know? The idea of being sixteen again, going back to the Sun Records rockabilly sound of Elvis and Buddy Holly. Playing old equipment—a hollow-body Rickenbacker, a stand-up bass. Our musical roots, really. The more we talked about it, the more we kept saying why not? So we got together with Derek and the drummer we'd been using, Corky Carroll, and found a fantastic sax player, Johnny Almond. We five formed Johnny Thunder and the Lightnings. We did everything as if it was still '57. We dressed in plaid jackets, bowties, and drainies. Greased back our hair. Jack found us a vintage motor coach and we toured the provinces in it, playing only small clubs, drinking scotch and Coke, smoking Woodies. No drugs. No Us songs. We pretended Us didn't even exist. Some people dismissed it all as a bleedin' stunt, but it was a gas for us. We even recorded the album live in the studio. *(laughs)* Never occurred to us it would be a smash.

Hoag: Its success set off the fifties nostalgia craze. You were also credited with making a statement—that rock music is theater.

Scarr: The most important thing it did was help us deal with the madness of the past few years. Rory and I began to turn those feelings into songs as we rode in the motor coach, like we had in the early days. That's where we wrote *New Age.*

Hoag: "Now is the time to turn the page/To stop looking back/To put away the rage/No more lonely nights/We're living in the new age." Were you?

Scarr: In a manner of speaking, yes. Tulip and I were back together, and happy. Musically, Rory and I were excited again. Excited by the new dance music sounds, like reggae and disco. Excited by the new technology in the studio. We couldn't wait to get in there. In many ways, *New Age* was our most satisfying album. It was an *up* album. We were up. Didn't last long, of course.

Hoag: What happened with Tulip?

Scarr: Violet happened. Tu just got incredibly protective after she had her. Wanted an entirely different life from the one we were leading, away from musicians and dirtiness. She put it to me just as the band was getting ready to tour America in support of *New Age:* Give it up, she said. Give it up or lose us. It wasn't a choice I wished to make, but she left me no alternative. She wouldn't budge. I-I simply couldn't give up the music. It was my life. So I lost her. Lost them. Greatest sacrifice I ever had to make for my music, but I made it. Never did live with anyone again. Couldn't. Tu got stranger and stranger after that. Discovered Himself. Got involved with that Reverend Bob and his pathetic little church.

Hoag: He used to deal drugs, the police found out.

Scarr: You don't say. Do they suspect him of killing her?

Hoag: I don't believe so.

Scarr: Have you heard anything from that Root person?

Hoag: No. It's my move now.

Scarr: Have you chosen it yet?

Hoag: I think so.

Scarr: (pause) I keep wondering if she suffered.

Hoag: It wasn't a pretty way to die, but I don't suppose there is one. I understand Jack buried her urn in the center of the maze.

Scarr: Yes. Violet planted tulip bulbs as a marker.

Hoag: That's nice . . . Let's talk about that last tour. I got a chance to watch the Kubrick movie.

Scarr: I never have, m'self. For obvious reasons.

Hoag: How did that come about?

Scarr: He approached us. Why not, we said—the more the merrier. Christ, it was already a monster production. Our own bleedin' plane. Truckloads of sound and lighting equipment. Wasn't long before we were all saying how sorry we were we'd given up on Johnny Thunder. Especially after Rory slipped.

Hoag: Slipped?

Scarr: He'd asked his Italian actress, Monica, to come with him. Instead of which she dumped him for Roman Polanski, who immediately put her in some movie he was making. Rory never did understand that people use each other, that people using each other is the entire basis of most human relationships.

Hoag: Including you and Tulip?

Scarr: I said *most*, mate. Rory didn't take it well. Got back into a bad-ass-rocker-on-the-road thing. Did coke and teenage girls by the ton. Snorted and performed. Snorted and fucked. Snorted and crashed. Snorted and started all over again. Never ate. I didn't know how he could do it. It would have broken me.

And it broke him, actually. He collapsed backstage after the Denver show and had to be put in hospital. We put out a statement saying the thin air had gotten to him.

Hoag: What were you doing while Rory was being a bad-ass rocker?

Scarr: (laughs) The truth? I wasn't a lad anymore. If I didn't follow a strict physical regimen I couldn't keep my wind up while I boogied around on those football arena stages. I had to jog two miles every morning. Get my rest. And as for the girls, I wasn't that interested in 'em anymore. They bored me. Had no minds of their own. No style. They were just shapely, empty receptacles, waiting to be filled. The fact is, Tulip had spoiled me for other women. She knew what she wanted. She had taste. Ideas. There'll never be another like her.

Hoag: Can we talk about the night Rory died?

Scarr: (pause) We were wrapping up "We're Double Trouble," our encore number, just as we had been every night on the tour. I noticed this flash down in front, but when I saw Rory fall, with blood coming from his nose, I thought it was the coke—he's bleeding from all of the snorting, I thought. Collapsing again, like in Denver. I was the last to know, you see. It wasn't until I saw that bugger waving the gun and heard Derek screaming that I got it. And then . . . then all I kept thinking was it's happening like with Puppy all over again. Only it *mustn't.* We mustn't lose Rory. "Why can't someone help him?" I kept wondering. "Why can't anyone help him?"

Hoag: You dropped your scouse accent up there.

Scarr: So I've been told. I have no recollection of that. I must have been in shock. When it finally hit me, when it sunk in that Rory was dead, I kept thinking—this will sound dreadful—I kept thinking it was a blessing. Rory died playing his guitar on a stage. He died the way he was meant to die. He was never meant to grow old, to become an aging wreck like I am. In so many ways he's better off . . .

Hoag: There are certain people, like Jim Morrison, whom you can't picture with gray hair. Rory is definitely one of them.

Scarr: Yes. Because he was the spirit of rock 'n' roll. Forever young. More wine, Hogarth?

Hoag: No thanks. I'm driving into town tonight.

Scarr: Business or pleasure?

Hoag: Neither.

Scarr: Ah, you've heard from Merilee then.

Hoag: Not exactly.

Scarr: *(pause)* Don't do anything you'll be sorry for, mate.

Hoag: Sound advice. You'll forgive me if I don't take it.

Scarr: Mates always forgive. If it works out between the two of you, I'd very much like to meet her. Bring her to the party, why don't you?

Hoag: Party?

Scarr: I'm giving a blowout a week from Saturday.

Hoag: Well, well. What's the occasion, Christmas?

Scarr: Who needs an occasion to say hello to a few hundred old mates?

(end tape)

CHAPTER TEN

Jack was in his office cleaning his Browning when I went out to fetch the Peugeot, his meaty bricklayers hands caressing the shotgun lovingly. A half-empty mug of stout sat next to his elbow on the desk. I watched him there from the garage for a second before he noticed me and nodded. I nodded back, and decided it was time to drop my hook in the water.

"Vi have other plans tonight?" I asked him casually from the office doorway.

Jack tried very hard to not register a reaction. He almost succeeded. "Miss Violet? I wouldn't know, sir." He kept rubbing his gun.

"Wouldn't you?"

"What are you suggesting?"

"You two are close, aren't you?" I patted myself on the flank. "Very close. . . ?"

I wanted a reaction. I got a reaction. First Jack put the shotgun down, which was nice. Then he got up, whirled, and cuffed me across the face with the back of his hand. My cheek went instantly numb. With his other hand, he grabbed me by the throat and slammed me against the wall and held me there, his purple face close to mine. His breath hadn't improved.

"Don't stick your nose in other people's business."

"Sticking my nose in other people's business *is* my business," I got out, hoarsely.

"Maybe you ought to change your business."

"Can't. Too old."

"You won't get much older if you don't back off. Got it?"

"I believe so. Yes."

He let me go. It wasn't until I felt the jolt of my heels that I realized he'd been holding me an inch or two off of the ground. He sat back down and finished his beer in one gulp. I stood there rubbing my neck. It felt like it had been squeezed in a bench vise. My cheek was burning where he'd hit me.

"Kind of touchy, aren't you, Jack?" I suggested gently.

He squinted up at me, like he'd gotten soap in his eyes. Then he dropped his head in his burly arms and began to weep. "She's m-making me *crazy*, Mr. Hoag," he sobbed. "Never in my life have I felt this way about any woman. I-I can't sleep. Can't eat. She's in my mind constantly. The smell of her is in my nostrils. She's so alive, so fresh . . . Christ, I-I'm going to *explode*!"

I took a seat and waited him out. When he was done crying, he wiped his eyes with the back of his hand and blew his nose into the gun rag he'd been using. It left an oily smear across his cheek. Then he held his hand out to me. I wish I could say I didn't flinch.

"I want to apologize for going after you, Mr. Hoag. Lost my head for a second. Sorry."

We shook. I said, "So what's the problem—is she going out on you?"

"She's *playing* with me. She won't get serious. I keep asking her to—"

"She's very young, Jack."

"Got a problem with that?" His voice was nasty again.

"Absolutely not. I'm in no way judging you—I just mean she may not be ready to get serious."

"I see." He nodded. "What should I do?"

"Who am I, Dr. Ruth?"

"Who is Dr. Ruth?"

"Give her time, Jack."

"I can't. This is it for me, Mr. Hoag. She's the one. We could have a life together here, she and I. A good life."

"Give her time," I repeated.

He lowered his eyes. "Did she . . . has she made a play for you?"

I cleared my throat. "A play for me?"

"She said she was in your room one night."

"Oh, that. Just acting frisky, I suppose. Besides, I'm involved with someone else. Somewhat. You don't have to worry about me, Jack."

"God bless you for that, Mr. Hoag."

"God has very little to do with it."

I patted him on the shoulder and left him there with his shotgun and his pain. He had about as much chance of settling down with Lady Vi as I had of being named chairman of the Federal Reserve. I think he knew it, too. But it didn't change how he felt. She was the one. That was all he knew.

Maybe I knew a little about what that was like.

The lights were on in the mews house. There was movement behind the shades. Zack was there. It had to be Zack. She would be at the theater now, onstage.

I sat there in the Peugeot, watching the shadow on the shades and thinking about Jackie Horner. Thinking about how he was feeling. Thinking about how I was feeling. Rotten things, feelings. Much better off without them.

Zack left a little before eleven. He's tall and lanky like I am, except he carries his shoulders stiffly, as if he's still wearing the hanger in his coat. The coat was a loden cloth. There was an Irish tweed hat on his head. He made sure the door was firmly shut before he headed out, hands buried deep in his pockets. He walked unsteadily. He was potted.

It would be easy, really. Just start up the Peugeot. Put her in gear. Pick up some speed. Run the pretentious asshole over. No one would ever know. It would be easy.

But no, that wasn't the crime I'd come here to commit.

I waited until he'd turned the corner before I got out and headed for her front door, fingering my key. I could hear a faint whooping noise from inside as I put the key in the lock. The whooping got downright loud when I made it inside and shut the door behind me. It was Lulu—tail thumping, ears flapping, she was hobbling toward me across the living room floor.

"Oh, I see," I said coolly. "So now you're happy to see me."

Not as happy as I was to see her. I picked her up and held her. She whooped some more and licked my nose and tried to crawl inside my trench coat. I stroked her and said some soothing, intimate things I won't bother to repeat here. Then I tried to put her down, only she wouldn't let me. So we investigated together.

This part wasn't so pleasant. His clothes were there in the bedroom. Brooks Brothers all the way. His toiletries were there in the bathroom. Ice-Blue Aqua Velva. Whew—no wonder Lulu was happy to see me. There were dishes in the kitchen sink they'd eaten from, glasses they drunk from. I'd hoped all of it would tell me something, like how the two of them were getting along, and where I stood. Maybe a real detective could read all of that from the evidence. I sure couldn't. I put Lulu down in her bed. She started to protest until I picked her and the bed up together and started for the front door. I opened it to find myself face to face with a real detective.

"Good evening, Hoagy," Farley Root said. He wore a belted black nylon raincoat and a scuffed black leather cap, and was jiggling one bony knee nervously.

"Good evening. Inspector," I said. "Merilee isn't here. She's at the theater."

"It's you I wished to speak with, if I may. And I'm not actually an—"

"No problem," I said, ushering him inside. "Just in the process of doing a little friendly dognapping. But how did you know I'd—?"

"I followed you here."

"All the way from Gadpole?"

"No, we've a team system. I picked you up not far from here."

I'd had no idea I was being followed. That tabloid reporter must have been clumsy. Clearly, Root and his men were not.

I put Lulu and her bed back down before the fireplace. She snuffled at me, confused by this change of plans. "Why follow me?" I asked Root.

"I like to know where everyone is. A fetish of mine. Hope you don't mind."

"As fetishes go it's not too terrible," I assured him. "Have a seat."

He took off his hat and coat and lunged for the love seat. He wore a plaid jacket and checked slacks. It was not an improvement over the green suit. "What happened to your cheek?" he asked.

"What, this old thing?" I fingered it gently. It had gotten red and tender. "It's nothing—just ran into a big hand. Whiskey?"

"Love one. Bit chilly out."

I poured two Laphroaigs and handed him one. He gripped the glass so tightly I thought he'd break it. I sat in the chair opposite him.

"Wondered if you'd ever received that inventory report," he said, swallowing the scotch over his giant Adam's apple.

"I did."

"And. . . ?"

I sipped the Laphroaig. No, it *was* too smoky for me. "And thank you."

He frowned, ran his gopher teeth over his lower lip. "You did say we would share information."

"I know."

He waited for me to offer him some. When I didn't, he narrowed his eyes at me coolly. "For your information, we've turned something up in regards to the Savile Row business. A lead slug. Twenty-gauge. A bus mechanic found it rattling about in the fuel filter of a bus he was servicing. There's a hole in the body of the bus where it entered. We checked its route sheets. It would have been in the approximate vicinity of Savile Row on that date and that approximate time. We can't be absolutely certain that it's from the attack upon you but . . ."

"We can assume it is."

"Yes."

I tugged at my ear. "Slugs, if I remember correctly, are used primarily in hunting preserves."

"That's right. As a safety precaution against accidents. A rifle bullet may carry as far as a mile across open ground, presenting a danger to hunters and game alike. Lead slugs have a far shorter range—two hundred yards perhaps. Fired from a shotgun."

"Any idea what kind fired this one?"

"Not possible. Slug's too chewed up."

"Too bad."

Still, I knew something now. I knew that Derek, a confirmed black powder man, hadn't shot me. That didn't necessarily mean he hadn't killed Puppy or Tulip. But he hadn't fired those shots on Savile Row.

Root drained his scotch. "My lord, this is excellent whiskey."

"You don't find it too smoky?"

"Not at all."

"Like some more?"

"Yes, but I'd best not. Work to be done."

That was his cue to get up and leave, but he just lingered there on the loveseat, watching me and sucking on his teeth, which didn't make a pretty sound.

"Okay," I finally said. "I do have something for you."

"Ah, good," he said, pleased. He took out his notepad and pen.

I suggested he check something out, something that couldn't be checked out without the kind of authorization he had and I didn't: the Church of Life.

"What about it?" Root inquired, making a careful note.

"Who bankrolls it—pays the rent, the upkeep, Father Bob's salary."

"What will that tell us?"

"Possibly nothing," I conceded. "Possibly a lot."

Possibly a whole lot, if what I was thinking turned out to be true.

"Very well," said Root. "I'll keep you informed." He put away his notebook and pen, got to his feet, and put on his coat, glancing over at Lulu, who was watching him from her bed. "You were having me on before about the dognapping, weren't you, Hoagy?"

"No, I wasn't, Inspector."

He started to say something, stopped. Started again. Stopped again. Then he went out into the damp night.

It may not be easy to compete with an ex-wife who happens to be perfect, but I did my best: when we returned to Gadpole, I took Lulu directly to the kitchen, where Pamela clucked over her and then cooked her up a spectacular platter of kippers and eggs. After she'd wolfed that down I carried her up to our rooms and positioned her before the fire on her leather chair. From there she gazed dreamily at the flames for about thirty seconds before her eyes drooped shut, her tail thumped once, and she was out.

I took a bubble bath myself. A light rain was tapping against the window now. After I toweled off I moved Lulu to the bed and got in with Irwin Shaw. She hobbled around me, then ensconced herself in her favorite position with a soft grunt of satisfaction.

The bedside phone rang the second I opened my book.

Merilee didn't say hello. "I assume you have her," was all she said, with a distinct lack of warmth.

"I do. And she's fine."

"This is a disgrace, Hoagy. An absolute disgrace. How could you?"

"I needed her, Merilee."

"You could have phoned. We could have worked something out. You didn't have to sneak in here like a thieving son of a sea cook."

"I really have missed your quaint little expressions."

"Explain yourself."

"I didn't want to be a bother."

"Try again. Martyrdom is not your style."

"You're right. Okay. I didn't ask you because I knew you'd say no and I'd give in to you, because I love you. Okay?"

She sorted her way through that one quietly for a moment. "Well . . . I suppose there's a kernel of honesty in there somewhere. Which is more than I can say for someone else I know. Or should I say used to know."

"Meaning?"

"The marriage is quite dead. We drove the stake through it over dinner."

My heart rate definitely picked up. "What happened?"

She sighed. "Nothing happened. I'm simply fed up with him blaming me for his problems, and with me blaming me. Not that I'm totally blameless, but at least I work at it. I try. He won't. He'd much rather look for excuses and villains. He can look elsewhere from now on. He's flying back to New York tomorrow. He's agreed to move out of the apartment immediately."

"Where is he now?"

"He checked into a hotel for tonight."

"Not Blakes, I hope."

"It hurts, darling. Something awful."

"I won't be a total hypocrite and say I'm sorry it didn't work out for you two. But I am sorry you're suffering."

"I came home from dinner in tears. All I wanted to do was hold my poor wounded sweetness."

"I needed her too. Sorry. Bad timing."

"When can I have her back?"

"Depends on the terms."

She was silent a moment. "I'm considering a package deal."

"Well, well. I guess this means I'm going to have to buy you a Christmas present."

"It most certainly does. Hoagy, darling?"

"Yes, Merilee?"

"Can we . . . can we make it work this time?"

"Of course we can. We're gifted, remember? We can do anything."

I hung up and settled back in the pillows with a contented sigh. Then I patted Lulu and reached for my book. Before I could open it I heard a rustling out in the hallway.

Lady Vi was going out early for her spanking.

When I heard her door shut I followed her to the top of the stairs and listened after her, just to make sure she wasn't scampering down to the kitchen for some warm milk and coming right back up. Silence. She'd gone outside by way of the pantry door. Good. Now was my chance.

I'd learned that she kept the door to the blue room locked when she wasn't in it. I'd also learned that Pamela kept copies of all of the room keys in a drawer in the kitchen. I had liberated the blue room key while Pamela was busy fixing Lulu's kippers. It was a big old-fashioned skeleton key. The lock was the kind you peep through. I let myself in.

The blue room wasn't exactly your typical room. For one thing, it wasn't blue—Violet bad covered the walls and ceiling with roll upon roll of aluminum foil. A nice decor statement if you want to feel like a Perdue oven stuffer-roaster. For another thing, there was very little in the way of furniture. A mattress placed directly on the floor minus box spring and frame. A dancer's bar bolted to one wall. A dressing table with a three-way mirror on it. There was nothing else. I headed for the dressing table.

She kept her loot in the bottom drawer. Here I found various wallets she'd stolen—one belonged to some Lord who owned a record company, another to the lawyer, Jay Weintraub, complete with credit cards and photos of his racehorses and two ugly kids. Violet had a thing for gold. Gold cigarette lighters, rings, bracelets, and coke spoons were heaped in the drawer. There was also a particularly lovely eighteen-carat gold Waterman fountain pen that I considered pocketing and returning to its rightful owner—me. But I thought better of it. I didn't want her to know I'd been in here.

Underneath all of this, I found what I was looking

for—snapshots. Tulip's snapshots. The ones Violet had made off with that time Tulip caught her messing around in her photo album.

The odds were not great that the photo that Tulip's killer had come for hadn't been in the album, that it had been right here. It was a long shot. But those are the ones to play—that's where the big payoffs are.

There was a snapshot of Tris and Rory sitting at a nightclub table with Brian Jones and Keith Richard—drinking, smoking, all of them looking incredibly young and arrogant. On the back Tulip had scrawled "Ad Lib Club, Oct. '65." There was one marked "Bournemouth, Aug. '66." Tris and Rory were on the beach, shirtless, comically flexing their puny biceps at the camera. Another, dated July '67, was of Tris, Rory and Derek feeding the bears in Copenhagen's Tivoli Gardens. And then there was another that . . .

There was another that was *it*—the photo I'd been looking for. The photo Tulip's killer had been looking for. The one that pulled it all together. Yes, it all fit now. Horrifyingly. So horrifyingly that I almost couldn't believe what I was looking at. But there it was, plain as can be. The truth.

The trick was going to be proving it.

CHAPTER ELEVEN

I'll give T. S. this—when he went social there was nothing small or shabby about it.

Delivery vans came and went for days before his party, crammed with cases of liquor, produce, meats, cheeses—enough to stock the QE2. Pamela directed the traffic, signed the slips, barked out orders, bartered. The last thing to arrive was a two-story-high spruce Christmas tree that rolled up to the front door on its own truck bed. It took a half dozen workmen to get it inside the mammoth grand ballroom and hoist it up. Tris's bodyguards were the ones who decorated it, twisting around on top of extension ladders as freely as their balance and their shoulder holsters allowed.

Everyone came. Bingo was there with his wife Barbara Bach. So were the McCartneys, Paul and Linda. Paul had gotten so cherubic he'd have made a fine Santa Claus. George Harrison, meanwhile, was starting to resemble Christopher Lee, the cadaverous British horror movie star. Keith Richard came with Patti Hansen, speaking of horror movies. Roger Daltrey came with short hair. Rod Stewart and Kelly Emberg were there. So were Steve and Eugenia Winwood, John McEnroe and Tatum O'Neal, Eric Clapton, Jimmy Page, Ron Wood, Stevie Nicks,

David Bowie, Michael Caine, Joan Collins, Pelé. Mick Jagger and Jerry Hall were not there. Andy and Fergie were. The press were kept out.

It was all quite civilized. The women wore shimmering gowns, the men raffish dinner clothes. The rough boys and girls had grown up. At least they had on the surface. Greeting them at the door were their host and hostess, T. S. and Violet. Tris was unusually charming and animated. He'd obviously had some chemical help. Vi was in a flirty, mischievous mood, which didn't bode well for Jack's evening. Neither did her outfit. She had on a black leather miniskirt, black boots, and a black leather vest. The vest was unbuttoned, and there was not a thing under it, unless you count the snake tattoo decal on her stomach. T. S., in contrast, was all in white—white suit, white shirt, white tie, white shoes.

I stuck with my basic tux. I never mess with a good thing.

"You don't do this sort of thing badly," I told T. S., when there was a brief lull in the arrivals.

"Thank you, Hogarth," he replied brightly. "Feels good to party again. Too much quiet is bad for a rocker's soul."

"You were right—all you had to do was pick up the phone."

He grinned at me, his eyes beady. Speed? Very likely. "Indeed," he said, "Indeed."

A stage had been set up in the colossal ballroom next to the big tree. On it a piano, organ, guitars and drums waited to be played. On long tables there were hams, turkeys, roasts, salads, puddings waiting to be devoured. I noticed a small shadow under the table where the bowl of jumbo shrimp was. Lulu was guarding it. Anytime someone approached it she would growl softly at them from under the table. The guest would frown, look around warily and then move on. No one had dared to touch the shrimp yet.

Jack was behind the bar in a red vest and green-and-red bow tie, dispensing punch and champagne, and keeping a protective eye on his feral young lady love.

Derek Gregg arrived with his companion, Jeffrey, both of them in maroon velvet dinner jackets. Jeffrey headed off to get them punch, leaving the former Us bassist alone with me for a moment.

"Quite a little coming-out party," Derek observed drily. "And such a cozy room."

"Something of a departure for him, it would seem."

"That's your influence," Derek said.

"My influence?"

"Yes. You've helped pull Mr. Cigar out of his shell. He's no longer afraid to show himself to people. You really ought to think about psychiatry, Mr. Hoag. As a career, I mean. You do amazing work." Derek shot a glance across the room. "Oh, dear, my Jeffrey's getting jealous. Will you excuse me?"

Marco Bartucci, the human teapot, came with two Middle Eastern gentlemen in dark blue suits, neither of whom he bothered to introduce me to. "Surprised to see me here, Mr. Hoag?" he asked, shaking my hand wetly

"A little."

"It's as I told you—we are all mates now. Life goes on."

"For some of us."

Marco mopped his forehead with a handkerchief. "Yes. The lucky ones."

"Meaning the ones who don't get caught?"

He narrowed his eyes at me. "I'm afraid I still don't much care for you, Mr. Hoag."

"Give me time. I'm an acquired taste, like raw oysters."

"Raw oysters make me quite ill. Slimy things."

"Funny, I should think you'd take right to them."

He bristled and stormed off. I really was going to have to work harder on my party chatter.

The guests provided the entertainment. Nothing formal. Just impromptu sessions among friends. Winwood, Clapton, Derek Gregg and Ringo fooled around up there for a while with "Louie, Louie," capping it off with an inspired rendition of Winwood's old Spencer Davis hit, "Gimme Some Lovin.'" McCartney straggled up there after Derek relinquished the bass. Then George Harrison was up there, too, chopping off some guitar chords. I peered closely at the stage and counted heads twice. No mistake—the three surviving members of the Beatles were performing "Twist and Shout" in Tristam Scarr's ballroom.

I don't usually like big parties, but this one wasn't terrible.

Merilee drove out in a borrowed car with a friend. They got there late, since they'd both been on stage that night. Merilee wore a new strapless black dress and her pearls. Her hair was piled atop her head in a Victorian-style bun, accentuating the strong beauty of her neck and bare shoulders. The friend was done up head to toe just like a twenties flappers. She didn't look even a bit silly.

"Hoagy darling, this is my friend Diana," Merilee said! "She's doing that Sondheim musical, and it turns out we have the same leg waxer and hate the same people."

Diana's hand was strong and cold, her smile radiant. I smiled back and said absolutely nothing, which I'd learned was the best way to avoid making a fool of myself whenever Merilee introduced me to an actress I'd had an adolescent crush on. It was hard to believe it had been more than twenty years since Diana Rigg played Emma Peel on *The Avengers.* She looked the same. I lie. She looked better.

I got them champagne from Jack, who was so distracted he didn't even notice me—Vi was on the dance floor hanging all over Steve Stevens, Billy Idol's guitarist. Poor Jack. I turned away, ran smack into Chris Reeve. Poor me. I had to listen, at length, to how he'd been puzzling over Superman's motivation in a scene they'd filmed that day.

"Superman has no motivation," I finally broke in. "He's a comic book character."

He weighed this a second. Then he thanked me profusely and charged off, nodding excitedly to himself.

Maybe I *was* getting better at party chatter. "Show me the maze, darling," Merilee begged me when I returned. Diana had wandered off. I found something useful to do with her champagne. "Don't you want to meet T. S. first?"

"Later."

"We'll get lost," I warned.

"We'll take Lulu—the vet said she should be exercising."

"Don't be mean.

"Who's being mean?"

I found Merilee's mink and my trench, and dragged Lulu away from the shrimp bowl, limping and protesting mightily. It was cold and crisp outside. Lulu trailed way behind us as we crossed the lawn, grousing vocally I had to urge her on with promises of unlimited shrimp, crab legs, lobster bisque. Floodlights ringed the maze entrance. I pulled up there.

"You're sure you want to go through with this?"

"Absolutely," Merilee replied.

We headed in, her hand on my arm, Lulu limping along behind. After two turns we'd all been swallowed up by it.

"Have you bought my present yet, darling?"

"Yes, I have."

"Goody. Can I have it tonight?"

"It's not Christmas yet."

I thought I heard a rustling sound in the hedge next to us.

"But this is a Christmas party," she argued. "Kind of"

It *was* a rustling sound. We were not alone. Someone was in the maze with us. Lulu heard it, too. She growled softly, moved up closer behind us. Merilee seemed not to have noticed. I took her hand, in case we needed to make a dash for it.

"Then tell me what you got me," she pressed.

"No."

"Please?"

"Merilee, I've never known anyone as kidlike about Christmas as you are." I glanced over at her. "You get anything for me yet?"

"We adults don't discuss such things," she replied, sticking her tongue out at me.

I heard it again. Louder. Next to us. This time Lulu charged, teeth bared, growling ferociously. It was a bunny wabbit. She chased it down the gravel path, limping not one bit, until it disappeared under the hedge. She barked a couple of times for good measure, then strutted back toward us, immensely pleased with herself. As soon as she got within ten feet of us she put the limp back on.

"Why, that little faker," marveled Merilee.

"I think she's been around the theater world too much," I observed.

"This is nice in here, isn't it? Let's buy a country place when we get back and plant one just like it."

"Consider it planted."

We continued strolling. As far as I was concerned we were seriously lost now.

"Are we playing, darling? At getting back together, I mean."

"I'm not playing, Merilee."

She looked over at me and sighed. "You'll have to wear black all of the time."

"I'll even wear black pajamas to bed at night."

"You will not."

She stopped and grabbed me. We kissed. Then she said, "Have you ever kissed anyone in a maze before?"

"I've never done anything in a maze before."

"A night for firsts."

I kissed her again. "And seconds."

We got a little cold waiting for one of the guards to come fetch us after I fired the flare gun from the strongbox, but we found plenty to keep ourselves occupied.

We went back in the house by way of the kitchen, so Merilee could meet Pamela. Amazingly, Pamela seemed unperturbed by the army of chefs, carvers and dishwashers running around her in high gear. The phone call I'd been waiting for came while the three of us stood there chatting. Pamela and Merilee continued to converse gaily as I stretched the phone cord into the pantry and swung the door shut behind me.

"Evening, Hoagy," Root said. "Sorry to disturb you in the midst of your seasonal celebrating."

There was a hint of excitement in his voice. "Quite all right, Inspector," I assured him.

"Actually, I'm—"

"What's up?"

"It's about that matter you suggested I look into. I've been able to learn the chief source of funding for the Church of Life. Traced it through the bank deposits. I take my hat off to you, sir. Some kind of hunch you had."

"So who is it?"

"Came to the church to talk to the reverend about it personally. I'm still here. He's dead, you see. Murdered. Another boning knife. This morning, by the looks of him. There wasn't much here of value, but what there was is gone. Same story as Tulip's. Place is quite thoroughly—"

"Who the hell is it?" I broke in. "Who financed him?" Root told me. Before he could ask me what it all added up to I quickly thanked him and hung up. Then I returned to the ballroom.

Violet was all over Jimmy Page now on the dance floor. This was not going unnoticed by Jack over by the punch bowl. I cut in. Delighted, she entwined her arms around my neck and we began to make our way around the dance floor, she gleefully rubbing her pelvis and her unencumbered breasts against me.

"You're sort of nice to dance with, y'know?" she said. "Our parts fit together just *so*."

"You're not so bad yourself."

For this I got her playful pink tongue in one of my ears, followed by an urgently whispered catalog of the various things she really felt like doing to me.

Jack wasn't missing any of this either.

"I think you're making Jack jealous," I said. She glanced over at him, then treated me to her tongue again. Other ear. "That all I'm doing?"

"You don't give up easily. I like that in a woman."

"Is that her?" she asked, indicating Merilee, who was deep in conversation across the room with Michael and Shakira Caine—and, fortunately, missing this.

"Yes, it is."

"She's very pretty."

"So are you."

"You really think so?" she asked, pleased.

"However, you're also a bad girl. You told Jack you slept with me that night you came to my room, didn't you?"

"No," she replied.

"Didn't you?" I repeated.

She pouted. "He jumped to conclusions."

"And you didn't bother to correct him."

"Why should I? He's the one who's crazy possessive. I mean, he's just crazy." She tossed her head petulantly. "So what if I let him think it? It's for his own bloody good. I mean, he's got to learn how to let up on a girl a little, y'know?"

"May I give you a little advice? It won't hurt a bit."

She shrugged. "Sure."

"Blow him off. Find yourself another playmate."

"Why should I?"

"I happen to know he's not very good at games.

I left her standing there on the dance floor with a confused pout, and went for some punch. Jack ladled it out for me, his eyes avoiding mine. His hands shook with jealous rage. I took the glass from him and stood there next to him, sipping from it.

"It was you who took those shots at me, wasn't it, Jack?"

His eyes stayed on the crowd. He said nothing.

"Don't bother to deny it," I said. "I know you did it."

He looked at me now. "How do you know?"

"Because I know what really happened now. I know who did the killings, and why, and that it wasn't you."

"H-How do you—?"

"Do me a favor, Jack?"

"Sir?"

"I'm going upstairs for a moment. Then out to the service garage."

"The garage?"

"Yes. I want you to tell someone that I've gone out there. I want you to tell that person I'm taking all of the notes and tapes I've made for Mr. Scarr's book to Inspector Root in London right away. That I think I've come upon something vital to do with the murders. I'll be taking the Peugeot, by the way."

"But why are you telling—?"

"Then I want you to phone Root at the Church of Life and tell him to get over here at once. I'll be in the garage, okay? Make sure you tell him that. Will you do this for me?"

"Yessir. Of course." Jack swallowed. "I'm . . . I'm truly sorry about what happened, Hoagy. I wasn't aiming at you, y'know."

"I know you weren't. If you had been you'd have hit me."

"She told me that you and her . . . that you two . . . I just wanted to scare you off. Get you out of here. That's all. I swear it. I followed you into London that day. Parked down the block from where you parked. Waited for you to come back. I-I've lost m'head. Plain lost it. I'm sorry. I'm so sorry."

I gave him a reassuring pat on the shoulder. "Not totally your fault. She sort of drove you to it. I won't hold it against you. But I should warn you that Lulu has been known to carry a grudge for years."

I drained my punch, which was a little too sweet, and handed Jack my empty glass. Then I told him who I wanted him to give my message to.

CHAPTER TWELVE

(Tape #8 with Tristam Scarr recorded in front seat of Peugeot station wagon, parked in Gadpole service garage, Dec. 16.)

Scarr: (voice indistinct) Where are you off to, Hogarth? Party's just getting exciting. Pagey's got Vi's vest off. She really has got a magnificent pair of—

Hoag: Some business to take care of in town.

Scarr: (voice indistinct) Right now?

Hoag: Writers work twenty-four hours a day, Tristam. Even when we're asleep our worst nightmares are supplying us with fresh material.

Scarr: (voice indistinct) And here I've gone and opened a bottle of champers for us. What a waste.

Hoag: Would that be Dom Perignon?

Scarr: (voice indistinct) I'm afraid so.

Hoag: Well . . . maybe you ought to hop in. It *is* awfully cold out there.

Scarr: (laughs) Indeed. *(Sound of car door opening, slamming shut. Voice much clearer now)* Nothing quite like the bubbly, is there?

Hoag: Nope. *(silence)* Ahh . . . It's particularly good at killing the taste of that punch. Here you go . . .

Scarr: I'd better hold off for a bit, actually. I'm afraid I'll pass out on my guests if I have any more. You go ahead.

Hoag: Don't mind if I do.

Scarr: Funny. I don't believe I've ever been in this car before.

Hoag: It's quite slow. But it gets there.

Scarr: And where is it going?

Hoag: You covered your tracks well, my friend.

Scarr: My tracks?

Hoag: Of course, getting shot at did throw me off for a while. I made the mistake of thinking that it was part of the big picture. It wasn't. It was just Violet messing with Jack's head. Funny thing is it was also Violet who helped me figure it all out. Your little girl really fouled things up for you, Tristam. It was she who stole the one piece of evidence that could give you away—the photograph. Tulip didn't have it. It wasn't in her album. I have it now. And as soon as I get into London, the police will have it. All of it. *(pause)* You know, it was Derek who had the keenest insight into you. He told me you are, at heart, an actor. I didn't realize just how gifted, how convincing an actor you are. Our entire collaboration has been one extended performance. All along, you've given me precisely what you thought I needed. I needed a bombshell, you gave me a bombshell—you told me someone had murdered Puppy. After I discussed it with the others I dismissed it as paranoid nonsense. But it wasn't that at all, was it? It was a shrewd ploy to push any suspicion off of yourself. Who would ever think *you* killed Puppy, especially if you were the one who brought the whole thing up in the first place? I needed intimate personal revelations, you gave me intimate personal revelations. Our breakthrough about your troubled childhood—a performance.

Scarr: You'd have quit that day if I hadn't given you that. You'd been shot at.

Hoag: Why didn't you just let me quit? You should have.

Scarr: I need a great book. You're the person who can give me one.

Hoag: Besides, you'd gotten away with all of this for so many years you figured you'd never get caught, didn't you? . . . *Rock of Ages* was the album that meant the most to *you.* It was the most you. And it was your first failure. You couldn't accept that. You couldn't accept that the critics hated it, that your fans hated it. Your swollen, drugged-out ego couldn't allow for that. So you blamed Puppy. It was *his* fault. It was because of *him* you couldn't tour-support it in America. That ate away at you. *Puppy* ate away at you. He got the attention, the acclaim, the stardom. Him, not you. Who the hell was he, anyway? Some black drummer. It drove you mad. "More for Me"—that's your personal anthem. More for me, me, me. That's been your anthem all along, hasn't it? *(silence)* Hasn't it?

Scarr: Go ahead and tell it.

Hoag: It was you who turned Puppy on to the supercharged speed at Rory's house that day. You couldn't risk buying it through Jack, so you got it from a scuzzy London drug dealer you knew, named Bob. Known lately as Father Bob. No one could find the pills at the time because you pocketed them. What did Puppy think, that you were taking some, too?

Scarr: Pup didn't care one way or the other. He'd have swallowed drain cleaner if he thought it would give him a rush.

Hoag: Things went along just great for you after that. With Puppy gone, you and Rory just got bigger and bigger. Became superstars. Millionaires. Idols. But there was always that one nagging problem between you, wasn't there? *Tulip.* Rory kept taking her away from you. Your oldest and best mate kept taking your woman away from you. She told me that no woman could mean as much to you two as you did to each other. She was wrong. Sharing her made you *crazy.* That's what was tormenting you when you lived out in Los Angeles. That's why you shot smack. Why you drank so much. You loved her. She was the only woman you ever loved. You couldn't stand having to share her with him. Having to share *everything* with him. The stage. The spotlight. The money. It was always the *two* of you. Rory and T. S. Double Trouble. *Us,* instead of *me.* But you couldn't kill *him.* Not like Puppy. So you split up. Only that wasn't so hot either. His solo album did great. You couldn't even finish one. You needed him. That was really hard for you to swallow. It put you in the hospital. But you did swallow it. You reunited, complete with hugs and kisses. Toured as Johnny Thunder and the Lightnings—mates, like the old days. No hoopla. No drugs. You could hold your feelings in check. Besides, you and Tulip were together again. Things were going good between you. Until she had the baby, and made you choose between her and your career. Poor Tulip. No way she could win that one. And then you and Rory went on your big '76 tour, and it all started coming back to the surface again, didn't it? The hate. The resentment. Especially when his coking got so heavy you had to start canceling shows. You freaked. Called up an L.A. acquaintance of yours from back in '68, when you hung out for a while there with Dennis Wilson. You reacted a little strangely when I referred to him one day while we were working. You went out of your way to insist you and Wilson had never been friends, it seemed odd to me at the time. But you had a very good reason. Because Dennis Wilson of the Beach Boys had a houseguest off and on in '68, a struggling musician named Charles Manson. Manson and his family stayed with Wilson. One of those family members was Larry Lloyd Little. The two of you got to know each other at Wilson's in October of '68. That's the date on the back of the picture Tulip took of you and Larry having a merry chat together. That's the photo you were looking for.

Scarr: You've got it back there with the other things, have you?

Hoag: Of course.

Scarr: May I? *(rustling sounds)* Oh, yes. That's it, all right. You didn't make a copy, did you?

Hoag: No.

Scarr: You wouldn't be lying?

Hoag: You're not thinking clearly, Tristam. If I was going to lie I'd say I *did make* a copy so you wouldn't be able to kill me yet. You'd have to track it down first. *(pause)* You are going to kill me, aren't you?

Scarr: Yes, I am. And your point is well taken. Do go on with the story. I'm fascinated.

Hoag: When the Manson family came to trial, Larry Lloyd Little became a witness for the prosecution. He got out in a few years. He was out in '76, when you decided Rory had to die. You convinced him to do it for you, and in a most dramatic fashion. How did you manage that? Did you tell him Rory was some kind of force of evil?

Scarr: (laughs) Nothing quite so complicated, Hogarth. Larry was a pimp. I paid him five thousand dollars.

Hoag: Figuring the police would gun him down on the spot.

Scarr: If they hadn't, I would have. I had a gun with me on stage, in case I needed it.

Hoag: You made Rory into a rock 'n' roll martyr. Kept him forever young. That's how you justify to yourself what you did. The truth is that he was your oldest and best mate and you had him murdered. But you've twisted the truth to suit you. You've twisted everything to suit you. That's what this memoir is all about—putting your lies down on paper so as to make them into truth . . . You had the limelight all to yourself now Rory was gone. Why did you give it up? Retreat here? And why are you choosing to come back now?

Scarr: What I told you before was true—I'd had it with the T. S. persona. I wanted to grow. I couldn't as long as Rory was around for me to fall back on.

Hoag: When you end a friendship, you really end it, don't you?

Scarr: It was necessary. As were the past few years I've spent alone here. I've been able to study, learn new instruments, experiment with new sounds . . .

Hoag: Everything was going fine until the day Pamela gave you my message about going to see Tulip's photo album. And something clicked. You'd forgotten about the one thing that could actually link you to Rory's murder. You'd forgotten about that photograph. And so had she. She hadn't looked in the album for years. She told me she couldn't. And she obviously didn't remember about you and Larry knowing each other.

Scarr: Her brain was quite thoroughly scrambled.

Hoag: Yes. It was all a blur, she said. Of course, there was always the chance she would remember. Enter your pal Father Bob. You'd been paying him off to keep quiet ever since he sold you the speed that killed Puppy. You even made his dreams come true. You set him up as a resident neighborhood guru. Financed his church, paid him a salary—it beat killing him. And it came in real handy when Tulip started getting into God in a serious way. You steered her right to him, just in case she did remember about Larry and felt like confiding in somebody evangelical. It was easy for you to manipulate her behavior. All you had to do was condemn him and she'd make a beeline right for him. He kept an eye on her for you. It turned out not to be necessary. Tulip never did remember about you and Larry Lloyd Little. Not until you came to see her and demanded that picture. Then she knew. And you had to kill her. You made it look like a break-in to confuse the police.

Scarr: (silence) I never wanted to kill her. But I had to—she said she would tell the police about me. She loathed me, you see, because Violet had left her for me. She blamed me for ruining Violet. *(pause)* I had to kill her.

Hoag: You played dumb when I mentioned her photo album on the way to the funeral. You said you had no recollection of it—just another facet of your fine overall performance. Except for one little slip. When I said she had photos from all over the place, including *Los Angeles*, there was a flicker in your eyes. You were wondering if somehow I knew. I didn't. But for an instant, you wondered. And you let it show.

Scarr: My guard was down. I was mourning the mother of my child.

Hoag: Whom you'd killed. And you didn't stop there. Things were in danger of unraveling now. The police knew that Father Bob had been a drug dealer. He was a loose end. He could talk. With Tulip dead there was no reason to keep him alive, so you killed him, too, and made it look like another break-in. Neat and tidy. *(pause)* I'm curious about the others. Derek, Marco, Jack . . . have they ever known?

Scarr: No. Never.

Hoag: They weren't aware you knew Larry Lloyd Little?

Scarr: They weren't around when I was mates with Dennis. I was on holiday after our tour. Just me and Tulip.

Hoag: But Jack was so opposed to my looking into the past. Why?

Scarr: He has a good life here with me. He was afraid you'd upset the present order.

Hoag: He was right.

Scarr: Yes.

Hoag: I thought I understood you, Tristam. Clearly, I didn't. I don't. Help me understand you.

Scarr: What for? You aren't going to finish our book.

Hoag: Indulge me—for friendship's sake.

Scarr: I don't expect you *can* understand me. Not by applying your morality to me.

Hoag: It doesn't apply to you?

Scarr: T. S. is not everyone else.

Hoag: You honestly think you're above the rules that we, as semicivilized people, set upon ourselves?

Scarr: Anyone who succeeds as I have—to the very top—has ignored those rules. They've lied, cheated, stolen . . .

Hoag: You've killed four people, Tristam. You're about to make it five. No one has a right to do that.

Scarr: You disappoint me, Hogarth. Being that you respect greatness, I thought you would appreciate what I've accomplished. I thought you would understand.

Hoag: (pause) "Whatever it takes . . ." That's what Derek said you were willing to do. I guess you've just gone—

Scarr: Farther than the others dare to go. Precisely. It's fear that brings the little people up short. They'd do just as I have if they had the balls. But they haven't, the poor sods. They're afraid they'll get caught. They're weak. I'm not. I've the balls to take what I want. *(pause)* And now, at long last, it's my time. A new image, thanks to the work you and I have done. New start. New sound. *Mine.* A double album, I think. A video. A return tour. The body isn't what it was, but otherwise I'm better than ever. Richer. Fuller.

Hoag: How do you live with yourself, Tristam?

Scarr: Whatever I've done has been necessary. It had to be done, or I wouldn't have done it.

Hoag: How nice. How very, very . . .

Scarr: (silence) You were saying?

Hoag: I was . . . I was just thinking how *comforting* it must be to be a psychopath . . . Kind of the ultimate form of self-indulgence, wouldn't you say?

Scarr: I've enjoyed our talks. I'll miss them.

Hoag: (silence) Yeah, I . . . Care for the last of the champers?

Scarr: You go right ahead.

Hoag: (silence) Must have had more to drink than I . . . Feeling kinda . . .

Scarr: Yes?

Hoag: Was getting fond of you, Tristam.

Scarr: Likewise.

Hoag: You were one of my idols. Haven't many left. Come to think of it, haven't any . . .

Scarr: Sorry if I disappointed you.

Hoag: How you going to do it?

Scarr: It will look like suicide.

Hoag: Why am I. . . ?

Scarr: Your failed writing career, I expect.

Hoag: Oh, that . . . Guess I'd buy it.

Scarr: And the police will as well.

Hoag: You know what I was thinking, Tristam? If everyone in the world was . . . was like you . . . the world would go to hell.

Scarr: Welcome to hell. Scarr's the name. Shall I take that empty bottle from you, Hogarth? *(silence)* Hogarth? *(Silence, followed by sound of car engine starting, then idling. Papers rustle. Car door opens, closes. Faintly, the sound of garage door sliding shut. Then the sound of engine idling.)*

(end tape)

CHAPTER THIRTEEN

"You could have been killed," fumed Merilee as she knelt there beside me, her brow creased with concern, her eyes big and shiny.

"I wasn't," I assured her, though I wasn't a hundred percent sure of it myself.

I was sitting on the gravel in front of the garage with my head throbbing. I was seriously groggy. Pamela kept waving spirits of ammonia under my nose and I kept waving them away. Lulu was watching me from beside Merilee, a low moan coming from her throat. From the main house came the sounds of music and laughter and voices. The party was still going strong.

"Up we go now, Hoagy," ordered Pamela, placing her hands under my arms and hoisting me none too gently to my feet. "We've got to keep you up and about or you'll be of no use to anyone.

She held onto one arm. Merilee took the other. The two of them began to walk me around the driveway on my rubbery legs.

"What if he'd had a gun?" demanded Merilee. "What if he'd just shot you instead of . . . of. . . ?

"I'd be dead," I replied. "The point is, I'm not. And I got him to show his hand. It's all on tape."

Root came out of the garage. He was shaking his head. It was Root who'd found me in the front seat of the Peugeot, out cold, about a half hour after T. S. had served me the drugged champagne and shut me in the garage with the car's engine running. It was Root who'd dragged me out into the fresh, cold air. He'd fetched the others at my request, after I started to come to.

"I don't see any tape recorder, Hoagy," Root said.

"I hid it under the driver's seat," I told him.

He nodded and went back in the garage. "Got it," he called, returning with the recorder. "Car is empty otherwise. He took your papers, tapes, all of it."

That was no problem. I'd made copies of everything, including the photograph. T. S. had bought my story that he was holding onto the only copy. It hadn't occurred to him I'd want him to kill me then and there—or to go ahead and try.

"Hoagy, darling?"

"Yes, Merilee?"

"Why *aren't* you dead?"

"Quite," agreed Pamela. "You should have died in there from the carbon monoxide."

"Oh, that. The Peugeot's a diesel. Can't kill someone from carbon monoxide poisoning by locking them in a garage with a diesel."

"Why not?" asked Root, frowning.

"Diesel engines don't produce carbon monoxide," I replied. "Or hardly any—not like gas engines do. The combustion systems are totally different. Diesel exhaust may be billowy and stinky, but it's also nontoxic. Not many people know that. I figured he didn't."

"How do *you* know it?" Merilee wondered.

"A French mechanic once told me."

"What if you'd misunderstood him?"

"I speak perfect French."

"I know, but—"

"You're saying you set yourself up?" Root asked, sucking on his gopher teeth.

I nodded, which I immediately regretted. It made something rattle inside my head. "He had to get me out of the way and he couldn't afford another murder, especially right here at his own home. That would keep things unraveling. So I gave him the perfect opportunity to stage a suicide. He put something in the champagne to knock me out. He didn't drink any of it himself, of course."

"Wouldn't the drug have shown up in your system?" asked Merilee. "I mean, if there'd been an autopsy?"

"Not necessarily, Miss Nash," said Root. "You'd be amazed at how many disappear quickly, and without a trace. Naturally, he took the bottle with him." Root turned to me. "He thinks you're dead."

"He thinks I'm dead."

"You really are a stupid ninny," said Merilee.

I took her hand and squeezed it. "Why, Merilee, that's one of the nicest things you've ever, ever . . ." My knees buckled.

"I think," said Pamela, grabbing me, "we'd best get some strong coffee into the lad."

Together, they walked me into Jack's apartment. I slumped into his lounge chair. Lulu vaulted into my lap, all pretense of gimpiness gone, and licked my nose. I really was going to have to wean her off of fish. Root lurched into the bedroom and closed the door behind him. He wanted to listen to the tape in private for some reason. Merilee sat across from me, wringing her hands. Pamela came in from the kitchen and pressed a steaming cup of instant coffee in my hand. I gulped from it. It didn't clear my head much, but it did burn my tongue.

"How do you feel, Hoagy?" Pamela demanded.

"I've felt worse, though I can't remember when offhand. And you?"

"Me?" Pamela asked.

"It must be a bit disturbing to find out you've been managing the country estate of a murderer."

"Believe me, it is not the first time."

I stared at her a second. "Pamela, I think I'm going to have to do your memoirs next."

"I'm afraid there won't be nearly enough spice."

"We'll make some up. That's where the fun comes in." Foolishly, I gulped some more coffee. "Not that this isn't my idea of fun."

The bedroom door opened. Root stood there in the doorway, his face ashen.

"All there?" I asked him.

"Dreadful stuff," he said quietly.

"Not a pretty story," I agreed.

"Dreadful stuff. All of those years . . . All of those lives . . ."

"What are you going to do, Inspector?" Merilee asked him.

"Do?" Root swallowed. "I-I'm going to go up there and arrest Tristam Scarr for the murder of four people."

"Don't forget the attempted murder of a fifth," I said. "I'll be happy to testify."

Root belted his trench coat, squared his shoulders, and started for the door. Abruptly, he stopped. "What am I doing? What *am* I doing? That's not some sewer rat up there. That's *T. S.*"

"A sewer rat," I added.

Root ran both of his hands through his messy carrot-colored hair. "But there are members of the royal family up there."

"They've gone," Pamela pointed out. "Another engagement."

Root pursed his lips, shot a glance at the phone. "Still. I'd best ring up headquarters first."

"Why, Inspector?" I asked.

"That's just it, you see. I'm *not* an—"

"You shouldn't be intimidated by people just because they're famous."

"I'm not," he insisted, reddening.

"Look at Merilee over there," I said. "She's as famous as anybody, and she's just plain folks."

Merilee stiffened. *"Just plain folks?"*

Root mulled it over, wavering. "I suppose you're onto something there . . ." He glanced at the phone again. Then he took a deep breath. "Well, then," he announced firmly, "I'm off." He started once more for the door. This time he opened it.

"Mind if I come with you?" I asked.

He pressed his gopher teeth into his lower lip. "Want to be in on the kill?"

"I want to see the look on his face."

We all went with him.

A major musical event was happening in the Gadpole ballroom. T. S. was performing up on the stage. It was the first time he'd been on any kind of stage in over ten years, and he was giving the performance of his life—wailing, shrieking, strutting, sweating. He had come out, all right. This was his new beginning. Fittingly, he'd chosen the very first Us hit, "Great Gosh Almighty." An all-star band was up there behind him—Jimmy Page on guitar, McCartney on bass, Charlie Watts on drums—but it was T. S. everyone was responding to. The dancing had stopped. The eating and drinking and talking had stopped. Each and every guest stood there clapping to the beat, cheering Tristam Scarr's return performance on until he finally brought the song home to a thundering finish, his hand-mike held up high as a triumphant salute.

And then they roared. It was a roar of approval. Of acclaim. Of love. He stood there, eyes agleam, and soaked it up. It was all for him. No one else. *Him.*

He had made it, at last.

He was so caught up in the moment that it took him awhile before he spotted me standing there before him with Root by my side. When he did his eyes widened. His face got very white. And then Tristam Scarr's body betrayed him.

It gave out.

Jack was the first to reach him when he toppled forward. Root got there right after him. Somebody started screaming. They couldn't bring him to. Root tried cardiopulmonary resuscitation on him. Pamela phoned for an ambulance. It was no use. T. S. was gone by the time it got there.

CHAPTER FOURTEEN

The story came out in waves in the press.

First, of course, came the shocking news that one of English rock music's most legendary bad boys had dropped dead in front of a couple hundred of the entertainment world's biggest celebrities. Then came the news that a police investigator, one Farley Root, had happened to be on the scene at the time. Then came the rest of it. Why Root was there. The confession tape he'd obtained. What had really happened to Puppy Johnson, to Rory Law, to Tulip, to Father Bob, and to me. Almost. A few days later came the results of the autopsy: Tristam Scarr had died of a heart attack brought on in part by a heavy dose of speed he'd taken shortly before his death—no doubt to get up for his performance. Evidence of advanced heart disease was also present. The drug and the strain of being onstage again had apparently been too much for him.

So had a certain unpleasant surprise.

I decided to stick around Gadpole until he was buried. I spent most of my time in my rooms trying to finish the job I'd come to do. But I couldn't seem to concentrate. Mostly, I just lay there on the leather sofa with a single malt whiskey in my hand, staring gloomily at the fire, Lulu dozing beside me in her chair. It was quiet up there, which suited me fine. I was not in a talky mood.

Our editor did call from New York to find out how much I had and how soon I'd have it—sooner being more commercially advantageous than later, of course.

"I really want that confession," he told me.

"You'll have it," I told him. "Does this qualify as topspin?"

"This," he replied happily, "is *heat*."

"Heat is better?"

"Listen, Hoag, did he really . . . are you sure he did all of that shit?"

"Quite sure."

"I can't figure it. A guy who has money, fame—has it all, you know?"

"Not quite. He didn't have it all to himself."

"Help us out, Hoag. Work with the lawyer, Weintraub. Otherwise he's liable to hold up the pub date for months. We're still talking about an authorized memoir here."

"I'm not writing an apology for what T. S. did."

"And we're not publishing one," he assured me. "Everybody here's been asking me . . . I mean, you spent all of that time with him. What was he like?"

I thought that one over. "Very bright. Very talented. Very unhappy. He was the Shadow Man. He lived by night. I had gotten to be sort of fond of him, actually."

"How do you feel about him now—knowing what he did?"

"I don't feel anything about him anymore."

I hung up and stretched back out on the sofa, thinking my answer sounded familiar to me. After a while I realized it was the last thing Tulip had said to me before he killed her. I guess T. S. had that effect on anyone who got close to him. Call it a form of self-preservation.

A small private funeral was held in the Gadpole chapel. Marco and Derek drove out from London for it. Jay Weintraub flew in from New York. A limo waited to take him right back to the airport. Pamela and Violet and Jack were there. I was there. A local cleric performed the service. The estate guards and a team of police reinforcements kept the press and T. S.'s fans from scaling the walls.

Afterward, Tristam Scarr was buried next to Tulip's urn in the center of the maze. Violet insisted on that. She stared, stone-faced, at the coffin as it was lowered. She did not cry for the man who had murdered her mother.

I left Gadpole the next day—clothes, papers and Merilee's Christmas gift all packed up. Before I left, Pamela informed me that Violet was inheriting everything that had belonged to her father, making her one of the richest teenagers in Great Britain. Pamela was being appointed her legal guardian, and for the time being would remain there at Gadpole with her.

"I'm sorry to hear that, Pamela," I said, as we stood there in the kitchen, saying good-bye. "Not that you've been named her guardian, but that you won't be coming back to the States with us."

She smiled, knelt and petted Lulu fondly. "One never knows. I just might come knocking on your door one of these days."

"And we just might let you in."

At that moment Violet came padding through in her ballet slippers, eating an apple and looking very bored.

"Bye, Vi," I said.

She nodded and kept on walking.

"Hoagy is *leaving*, Violet," Pamela pointed out.

She nodded again and kept on going out the door. We looked after her.

Pamela shook her head. "She's really not a bad girl, you know. The poor dear just needs some normalcy in her life. It's not something she's gotten very much of."

Something told me Pamela would see that she got plenty of it.

I found Jack in his garage apartment, packing his bags.

"Pam has asked me to stay and help her look after things," he told me, "But I think it best I move on."

"What about you and Violet?"

Jack squared his jaw grimly. "She's an heiress now, Mr. Hoag. She'll be a great lady one day. She doesn't need the likes of me around."

"Where are you heading?"

"I don't know, sir."

I stuck out my hand. "If you find yourself in New York, look me up. I'll get you drunk. No charge."

He shook it. "That's damned kind of you, considering."

"Let's just say I've been there."

"Mr. Hoag?"

"Yes, Jack?"

He looked down at his feet. "Will I get over her?"

I managed a reassuring smile and said, "You'd be surprised."

"Yes," he said gravely. "I would be."

Root happened by to take some final statements. I bummed a lift into London off of him.

"Terribly sorry about the way the newspapers made this affair appear Hoagy," Root said, as we eased down the long driveway in his Austin, my stuff stowed in the trunk.

"How did they make it look?" I asked.

Lulu sat in my lap, longingly watching Gadpole recede through the window. She'd liked it there.

"As if I . . . well, you and I know it *was you* who made the important breakthroughs in this case."

"I wouldn't say that, Inspector."

"Actually, I'm not an—" Root stopped himself, glanced over

at me with a pleased, buck-toothed grin, then turned back to the road before us, still grinning.

"Don't tell me you made it," I said.

"I did."

"Well, well. Congratulations, Inspector. I knew it was just a matter of time."

"Thank you, sir. For everything."

The guards opened the gate and let us through. I waved good-bye. They didn't wave back. When we hit the main road I decided it was time to give Root the name of my tailor.

I had my introductory chapter now, the one that sets the tone of the memoir. It wasn't exactly the tone I'd been expecting earlier on, but you seldom get what you expect in my business.

I wrote it over the next few mornings at the mews house while Merilee slept. I worked at the dining table, with a fire crackling in the fireplace and Lulu asleep under my chair, her head on my mukluk. I wrote it in my own voice. I had to. The reader had to know what had transpired since I'd begun my collaboration with Tristam Scarr. Had to bear in mind that the story they were about to read was his own version of his life, and of history, and that there was another version. I covered that version in a final chapter that was also written in my voice. In it I detailed the murders, past and present, his attempt on my life, his confession, and his own death onstage at his coming-out party.

I didn't think it made for dull reading, but that's just my opinion. You'll have to make up your own mind.

The day that I put it in the mail to New York happened to be the same day Merilee finished her run in *The Philadelphia Story*. It also happened to be Christmas Eve. We celebrated all of these things with Lulu at the Hungry Horse. The waiter remembered us. He didn't have to be told to bring us a bowl of olives to go with our martinis.

Merilee seemed drained and a little down. She usually does when the curtain has just fallen on a role for the last time. That was something I understood. I felt pretty much the same way that night.

"Glad to be finished, darling?" She mustered a weary smile as we clinked our glasses.

"It was a hard one. I lost a little of myself this time. I guess that's what happens when you lose an idol. That and you get bitter. I don't want to get bitter. I don't want to become someone who just sits there waiting for the bad to surface in other people. And in myself." I drained my martini. "I keep thinking I really don't want to do this kind of work again."

"Go back to work on your novel. That's what you need to do."

"I intend to." I caught the waiter's eye and ordered us another round. "I miss New York. Tomorrow too soon to head back?"

She cleared her throat, looked away uneasily. "Something rather sudden has come up, actually. My agent called. I've . . . I'm taking this film role."

I tugged at my ear. "Film role?"

"They're already in production. In Tunisia," she said, the words tumbling out quickly. "See, they wanted Meryl, and they thought they had her, only her deal fell through at the last minute and, well, it's quite a plum for me, even if I'm not exactly their first choice. It's a Graham Greene thing. Pinter adapted it. Jimmy Woods is the male lead, and the director is—"

"Feel like some company?"

She examined the tablecloth for a full minute, her lips pursed. Then she shook her head.

The waiter came with our drinks and asked if we were ready to order. Somehow the thought of rare meat wasn't quite as appealing as it had been five minutes before. I waved him away.

"I-I need to be on my own for a while, darling," she began. "The past few weeks—they've been wonderful. Special. But something just isn't right with me. I've gone from you to Zack, then from Zack right back to you again. I keep messing things up. I need to be on my own for a while. Figure things out. No messes. I . . . I'll be home in a few months, okay?"

"Okay," I said, knowing she wasn't coming home, at least not to me she wasn't. What had happened between us over the past few weeks was finished. It had been London. It had been Tracy. It had been . . . hell, who knew what it had been. Whatever, it was done. For now.

"I'm so sorry, darling. Really, I am."

Her green eyes were brimming now. I got lost in them.

"Don't be sorry," I said. "We had a terrific time. We'll have other terrific times. And we'll have them soon. You're mine. You always will be mine. I'm quite sure of that." I drained my drink, glanced at Lulu in Merilee's lap. "I'm afraid it's going to be tough on you-know-who, though."

"On me, too," she said, stroking you-know-who's ears. "You don't have to wait for me."

"I know I don't. But I will."

"So understanding," she said, covering my hand with hers. "So very, very understanding."

"That's me, all right. Of course, this means you don't get your Christmas present now."

"What?"

It was a shawl-collared cardigan sweater made out of eight-ply oyster gray cashmere. A men's size forty-two. My size. I'd picked it up in the Burlington Arcade one afternoon, knowing it would look like a million bucks on her.

I wore it home on the plane. I figured I may as well start

breaking it in right away, so it would be good and ready for her when our time came again.

The plane was nearly empty. Not many people fly on Christmas Day. Lulu didn't stop whimpering during the whole damned flight, even though I let her eat my seafood cocktail.

ABOUT THE AUTHOR

David Handler (b. 1952) is the critically acclaimed author of several bestselling mystery series. He began his career as a New York City reporter, and wrote his first two novels—*Kiddo* (1987) and *Boss* (1988)—about his Los Angeles childhood. In 1988 he published *The Man Who Died Laughing*, the first of a series of mysteries starring ghostwriter Stuart Hoag and his faithful basset hound Lulu. Handler wrote eight of the novels, winning both Edgar and American Mystery awards for *The Man Who Would Be F. Scott Fitzgerald* (1990).

The Cold Blue Blood (2001) introduced a new series character, New York film critic Mitch Berger, who fights his reclusive nature to solve crimes with the help of police Lieutenant Desiree Mitry. Handler has published eleven novels starring the pair. He lives and writes in Old Lyme, Connecticut.

THE STEWART HOAG MYSTERIES

FROM MYSTERIOUSPRESS.COM
AND OPEN ROAD MEDIA

MYSTERIOUSPRESS.COM

MYSTERIOUSPRESS.COM

Otto Penzler, owner of the Mysterious Bookshop in Manhattan, founded the Mysterious Press in 1975. Penzler quickly became known for his outstanding selection of mystery, crime, and suspense books, both from his imprint and in his store. The imprint was devoted to printing the best books in these genres, using fine paper and top dust-jacket artists, as well as offering many limited, signed editions.

Now the Mysterious Press has gone digital, publishing ebooks through **MysteriousPress.com**.

MysteriousPress.com offers readers essential noir and suspense fiction, hard-boiled crime novels, and the latest thrillers from both debut authors and mystery masters. Discover classics and new voices, all from one legendary source.

FIND OUT MORE AT

WWW.MYSTERIOUSPRESS.COM

FOLLOW US:

@emysteries and Facebook.com/MysteriousPressCom

MysteriousPress.com is one of a select group of publishing partners of Open Road Integrated Media, Inc.

THE MYSTERIOUS BOOKSHOP, founded in 1979, is located in Manhattan's Tribeca neighborhood. It is the oldest and largest mystery-specialty bookstore in America.

The shop stocks the finest selection of new mystery hardcovers, paperbacks, and periodicals. It also features a superb collection of signed modern first editions, rare and collectable works, and Sherlock Holmes titles. The bookshop issues a free monthly newsletter highlighting its book clubs, new releases, events, and recently acquired books.

58 Warren Street
info@mysteriousbookshop.com
(212) 587-1011
Monday through Saturday
11:00 a.m. to 7:00 p.m.

FIND OUT MORE AT:

www.mysteriousbookshop.com

FOLLOW US:

@TheMysterious and Facebook.com/MysteriousBookshop

www.ingramcontent.com/pod-product-compliance
Lightning Source LLC
LaVergne TN
LVHW090604110826
845146LV00001B/252

* 9 7 9 8 3 3 7 2 0 5 4 3 4 *